OF HARUHI SUZUMIYA

Rampage

NAGARU TANIGAWA

YEN ON
NEW YORK

The Rampage of Haruhi Suzumiya
Nagaru Tanigawa

Translation by Chris Pai for MX Media LLC
Cover art by Noizi Ito

Suzumiya Haruhi No Bōsō
©Nagaru Tanigawa, Noizi Ito 2004
First published in Japan in 2004 by KADOKAWA CORPORATION, Tokyo.
English translation rights arranged with KADOKAWA CORPORATION, Tokyo,
through TUTTLE-MORI AGENCY, INC., Tokyo.

Yen On
150 West 30th Street, 19th Floor
New York, NY 10001

Visit us at yenpress.com
facebook.com/yenpress
twitter.com/yenpress
yenpress.tumblr.com
instagram.com/yenpress

First Yen On Edition: March 2021
Previously published in paperback and hardcover by Yen Press in June 2011.

Yen On is an imprint of Yen Press, LLC.
The Yen On name and logo are trademarks of Yen Press, LLC.

The publisher is not responsible for websites (or their content)
that are not owned by the publisher.

The Library of Congress has catalogued the hardcover and previous paperback as follows:
Tanigawa, Nagaru.
[Suzumiya Haruhi no boso]
The rampage of Haruhi Suzumiya / Nagaru Tanigawa ; [English translation by Chris Pai].—1st U.S. ed.
p. cm.
ISBN 978-0-316-03882-9 (hc) / ISBN 978-0-316-03884-3 (pb)
[1. Supernatural—Fiction. 2. Clubs—Fiction. 3. Japan—Fiction.] I. Pai, Chris. II. Title.
PZ7.T16139Ram 2011 [Fic]—dc22
2010043276

ISBN: 978-1-9753-2287-8

1 3 5 7 9 10 8 6 4 2

LSC-C

Printed in the United States of America

The Rampage
OF HARUHI SUZUMIYA

NAGARU TANIGAWA

First released in Japan in 2003, *The Melancholy of Haruhi Suzumiya* quickly established itself as a publishing phenomenon, drawing much of its inspiration from Japanese pop culture and Japanese comics in particular. With this foundation, the original publication of each book in the Haruhi series included several black-and-white spot illustrations as well as a four-page color insert—all of which are faithfully reproduced here to preserve the authenticity of the first-ever English edition.

CONTENTS

PREFACE · SUMMER

This story happened back before the sigh-filled movie shooting, during our high school's long summer vacation.

It was a few days after returning from the SOS Brigade's summer camp, the staged mystery ordeal on the remote island, and I was finally beginning to enjoy my summer vacation.

After all, I'd practically been dragged in chains to the so-called camp by our impatient brigade chief on the first day of summer vacation, which put a dent in my meticulous plans for sleeping past noon on the first few days of vacation without anyone yelling at me. This was why my body wasn't able to switch to summer vacation mode until July was nearly over.

I shouldn't need to tell you that I was unable to muster the willpower to tackle the mountain of homework. Hey, I just figured I could put it off till August, so I took it nice and easy, and the next thing I knew, July was already over. Once we hit August, I accompanied my impressively hyper little sister, hopping and skipping all over the place, to the countryside to visit the cousins, nephews, and nieces we hadn't seen in a while for two weeks of rivers, beaches, mountains, and prairies. Such a satisfying experience that I wanted to brag about it to someone.

Naturally, I was avoiding the homework I didn't want to do the same way birds learn to avoid poisonous larvae. As a result, day after day passed on the calendar without a single question's being answered, and before I knew it August was already half over...

That was when "it" began without anyone noticing...

Or so I hear.

ENDLESS EIGHT

Something was wrong.

I first began to notice on a fine summer day after the Bon Festival.

At the time I happened to be lounging around the living room watching a high school baseball game on TV without being particularly interested. I'd accidentally woken up before noon, so I was pretty bored, though not bored enough to feel like attacking the mountain of summer homework awaiting me.

The game on TV, between schools from the same district, had nothing to do with me, but the spirit of rooting for the underdog made me cheer for the team on the losing end of the 7–0 score. For some unknown reason, I just had a feeling that Haruhi was about to make trouble.

I hadn't seen Haruhi in a while. I'd taken my little sister to the countryside, where my mom had grown up, to beat the heat and pay our respects to our ancestors, and we'd only returned the day before. This was an annual practice that couldn't be skipped, but then it was summer vacation, so it was only natural that there really weren't many chances to run into any SOS Brigade members.

Besides, we'd already been through the bizarre happenings when we went to that crazy island, aka the SOS summer camp, back when summer vacation had barely started. I was pretty sure that even Haruhi wouldn't suggest a second trip. She should have been satisfied by now.

"Anyway."

I sighed as I tugged my silent cell phone toward me by the strap ever so casually when something happened to make me wonder if there were any hidden cameras in the room.

My phone began to ring with what could only be considered perfect timing. For a moment, I thought I'd become prescient, but I immediately shook my head and abandoned the idea. Idiotic.

"What is it?"

The name displayed on the phone was none other than Haruhi's.

I waited three rings before slowly pressing the Talk button. I had a feeling that I already knew what she was going to say, which made me want to question my sanity.

"You're free today, right?"

That was the first thing out of Haruhi's mouth.

"We're all meeting up in front of the station at two. You better come."

And with that, she hung up. No seasonal greeting, not even a simple hello. And she didn't even check to make sure that I was the one who had answered the phone. Besides, how did she know I was free today? I'm actually quite . . . well, I suppose I have no plans at all.

The phone rang again.

"What?"

"I forgot to tell you what to bring."

She quickly rattled off the necessary items.

"You'll need to come on your bicycle. And have plenty of money. Over."

She hung up.

I tossed the phone down and tilted my head. Why do I have this funny feeling, like I'm still dreaming?

A soft cheer came from the television and I turned to find that the team I'd mentally designated the opposition had reached double digits. The ringing sound of baseballs against aluminum bats made that very clear.

Summer was almost over.

I could hear a chorus of chirping cicadas from my vantage point in this tightly sealed room with the AC on at full blast.

"Guess I have no choice."

Still, hadn't Haruhi been satisfied by the so-called summer camp at the beginning of our break when she took us to that weird island? What are we supposed to do in this suffocating heat? I don't feel like moving an inch from my nicely air-conditioned room.

And with that thought, I headed to my closet to assemble the required items.

"You're late, Kyon. You need to show some more effort!"

Haruhi was swinging a vinyl bag around as she jabbed a finger at me with a grumpy look on her face. I see that she never changes.

"Mikuru, Yuki, and Koizumi were all here before I was. Who do you think you are to keep the brigade chief waiting? You get a penalty! A penalty!"

I was the last one to arrive at our meeting place. I came fifteen minutes early, but the other members had moved even more quickly, as though they had been expecting Haruhi's call. This was why I always ended up having to pay, but I was used to that by now. I was just an ordinary human. I had no chance of jumping the gun on three people with such special backgrounds.

I ignored Haruhi and raised my hand in greeting toward the earnest brigade members.

"Sorry to keep you waiting."

The other two aside, there was one person I needed to apologize to. Mikuru Asahina, adorned with a fancy ribboned hat, flashed me a soft smile as she bowed her head.

"It's okay. I just got here myself."

Asahina carried a basket in her hands. I had a feeling that there were good things inside, which got me all excited. I wanted to savor that feeling a little longer, but I was interrupted by a voice next to me.

"It's been a while. Did you go on another trip afterward?"

Itsuki Koizumi revealed his glistening white teeth as he gave me a thumbs-up. His suspicious-looking smile hadn't changed after over half of summer vacation's passing. You should have gone on a trip yourself. Why did you instantly respond to Haruhi's summons? There's no end to the questions I could ask. Learn how to say no.

I bypassed Koizumi's phony cheerful face and turned my eyes to the side. Yuki Nagato stood there blankly, as though she were Koizumi's artificial shadow. She stood in her summer uniform without a drop of sweat to be seen, a very familiar sight. I had to wonder if she even had sweat glands.

"…"

Nagato looked up at me as though she were staring at a motionless toy mouse and tilted her head slightly. Was that supposed to be a greeting?

"Well, everybody's here. Let's get going."

Haruhi raised her voice. I felt obligated to ask.

"Where to?"

"The public pool, obviously."

I looked down at the duffel bag in my right hand, which contained a towel and swim trunks. Well, I knew that we would be heading for some pool.

"You're supposed to do summerlike activities in the summer-time. Only swans or penguins would enjoy swimming in the middle of winter."

They spend the entire year in water, and they don't particularly seem to enjoy themselves. I'm not the kind of person to accept an irrelevant comparison in an argument.

"Time never comes back once it's gone. So we have to do this now, during our only summer as freshmen in high school!"

Haruhi was in her usual rhythm with no intention of listening to what anyone else had to say. The other three members never bother wasting their time on offering Haruhi an opinion, which meant that I was the only one whose suggestions went ignored. From a rational point of view, that was pretty unreasonable, but I was the only rational person here, so this was apparently my fate. Not much of a fate.

I began pondering the difference between fate and destiny.

"We're going to the pool by bicycle."

Haruhi announced her plan and proceeded to put it into action, despite the fact that nobody had agreed to it.

Upon asking, I learned that Koizumi had also been told to come on his bicycle. The three girls had walked here. I should mention that there were a total of two bicycles. The SOS Brigade had five members. Well, how does she intend to solve this problem?

Haruhi's answer came in a cheerful voice.

"We can have two ride one bike and three ride the other. Koizumi, you're carrying Mikuru. Yuki and I will ride behind Kyon."

And so I found myself frantically pedaling away. I could deal with the sweltering heat and dripping sweat, but something needed to be done about the incessantly yapping voice behind my head that sounded like a speakerphone with a busted volume control.

"C'mon, Kyon! Koizumi's getting ahead of you! Pedal harder! Pick up the pace! Blow by him!"

Through my hazy vision, I could see Asahina wave shyly at me from her position sitting sideways on the rack of Koizumi's bicycle. How come Koizumi gets that and I'm stuck with this? I had to wonder if the word "unfair" had originated from the very situation I was in.

My bicycle and legs were struggling to endure this crippling load. Nagato was sitting on the rack while Haruhi was standing on the hub of the back wheel and holding on to my shoulders, a somewhat acrobatic way for three people to ride together. When did the SOS Brigade become a circus?

Incidentally, Haruhi said the following before we departed:

"Yuki's so small that she's practically weightless."

That was, in fact, the case. I don't know if she set her own weight to zero or used some kind of antigravity trick, but I could feel only Haruhi's weight as I pedaled away. Well, I wasn't particularly surprised by the fact that Nagato was manipulating gravity. Hell, I'm more interested in finding out what she isn't capable of doing.

I wouldn't have had any complaints if she could also have done something about Haruhi's weight, but I could still feel her against my back.

I could see Koizumi peering back at me over Asahina's head while trying to hide that irritating smile of his, leaving me to lament in a Balzacian manner. Like the writer, I pondered how hilariously unjust our world was. Damn, I absolutely have to enjoy the experience of riding with Asahina. I'm sure that my granny bike felt the same way.

The public pool was so shoddy that it might as well have been called a communal pool. After all, there were only a 150-foot pool and a six-inch-deep pond for little kids.

The only high schoolers who would come to swim at this pool were the ones who couldn't find anywhere else to go, or, in other words, us. There were only kids and their parents—mothers, for the most part—around. I took one look at the crush of kiddies in their swim rings and immediately lost interest. It appeared that Asahina would be the only one to entertain my optical sense.

"Yep, the smell of chlorine. It really brings out the atmosphere."

Haruhi stood under the sun in a crimson tankini and sniffed at the air with her eyes closed. She exited the changing room with a firm grip on Asahina's hand. Asahina, with her basket in one arm, was dressed in a childish, frilly one-piece, while Nagato was in some kind of plain racing swimsuit. Haruhi probably chose their swimsuits. She didn't give a damn about her own attire, but she tended to make a fuss about what other people (especially Asahina) were wearing.

"Anyway, let's find a place to dump our stuff. Then we can go swim. Let's race. See who can swim from one end to the other the fastest."

And after making that juvenile proposition, she jumped into the pool without any stretching. Can't she read the NO DIVING signs all over the place?

"Hurry it up! The water's all warm and comfortable!"

I shrugged and exchanged a look with Asahina before walking toward a nearby patch of shade to set down my towel and bag.

There were kids littered across the surface of the water like an outbreak of water striders, making it impossible to swim in a straight line. The brigade members were forced into a fifty-meter freestyle race under these harsh conditions that yielded a surprising result, or not really, I guess. Either way, the first person to reach the other side was Nagato.

Apparently she swam the entire length submerged, without ever coming up for a single breath. She waited at the goal with water dripping from the strands of her short hair that were stuck to her face as she silently watched us arrive. It goes without saying that Asahina was last. She had to stop every time she took a breath and throw back a beach ball that happened to land nearby before finally reaching the other side, after taking ten times as long as Nagato had, by which time she was completely out of breath.

"The idea of using sports to blow off stress is just a sham. Your body and mind are separate. I mean, you don't have to think for your body to move, but you have to think for your mind to work."

Haruhi had a look on her face like she'd just said something profound.

"That's why we should race again. Yuki, I won't lose this time!"

Didn't an adult ever teach her that you're supposed to make sense when you talk? What kind of logic was that? You just don't want to lose. It'll be a contest of endurance until you win.

That was why I hoped Nagato would understand the situation as I hauled myself out of the pool. The two of you can race by yourselves. I'll be sitting by the pool as a spectator. My money's on Nagato. Anyone want to bet on Haruhi?

Haruhi and Nagato made the fifty-meter swim five more times in both directions before the three female members of the SOS Brigade joined a group of grade-schoolers nearby who happened to be playing with a ball. Koizumi and I, bored out of our minds, could only watch as the girls played in the water, since there was nothing else to do.

"They seem to be enjoying themselves."

Koizumi continued to watch them as he spoke.

"Quite a pleasant sight. And it feels peaceful. Wouldn't you agree that Suzumiya is learning to have fun in a normal fashion?"

He seemed to be talking to me, so I responded.

"I wouldn't consider calling me with no warning and hanging up the second her business was finished a normal way to invite some-one."

"As they say, there's no time like the present to act on an idea."

"Has she ever hesitated to act on an idea the second it's out of her mind?"

Images of the ridiculous baseball game and giant cave cricket flashed through my mind.

Koizumi smiled.

"Nevertheless, this would be considered relatively peaceful. There shouldn't be any earthshaking events when Suzumiya has such a cheerful smile on her face."

Sure hope you're right.

I'm not sure how he interpreted my exaggerated sigh as he chuckled with a snort—

—That was when Koizumi got a weird look on his face. One I wasn't accustomed to. In other words, he didn't have that thin smile.

"Hmm?"

Koizumi's brow creased.

"What's wrong?" I asked.

"Nothing…"

Koizumi appeared to be tongue-tied, a rare sight, but he soon recovered his smile.

"Probably just my imagination. I must have become a little over-sensitive after everything that's happened since spring. Ah, they're coming out of the water."

I looked in the direction Koizumi was pointing to see Haruhi walking over like an emperor penguin bringing food to its chicks, with a wide smile on her face. Asahina and Nagato trailed after her like servants accompanying a princess who was running away from the castle.

"It's almost time to eat. Guess what? Mikuru made sandwiches. You could sell them on the street for five thousand yen or auction them off for at least five hundred thousand. But you get to eat them for free, so you should be grateful."

"Thank you very much," I said to Asahina.

Koizumi followed my lead and bowed his head.

"How very kind of you."

"It was nothing."

Asahina looked down shyly as she fidgeted with her fingers.

"I don't know if I did a very good job…I apologize if they taste bad."

That would be impossible. Any food that's been graced by the touch of Asahina's hands is guaranteed to taste delicious. In this case, the "who" part of 5W1H would take priority.

Hence, I was so overwhelmed by the privilege of enjoying Asahina's assorted handmade sandwiches that I wasn't sure how they tasted. Anything would do at this point. The hot Japanese tea she poured us didn't go very well with the sandwiches, but that was no problem at all. Even her sweat appeared refreshing to my soul.

Haruhi quickly devoured her portion before standing up like she needed to let out the heat built up in her body.

"I'm going back for another swim. You can all join me when you're done eating."

And with that she dived back into the pool.

I'm impressed by how she's able to swim so smoothly in a place with so many obstacles. The theory about humans originating from the ocean might have some merit. Though I would expect Haruhi's distant ancestors to be capable of adapting to the moon if they were sent there with only the clothes on their backs.

Sometime later Nagato, still eating slowly in silence, was left behind as the other three of us headed for Haruhi, who was prancing around in the water like a seal seeking a mate. By this point Haruhi was having fun with a group of grade-school girls playing underwater dodgeball.

"Mikuru, get over here!"

"Yes!"

Asahina nodded leisurely before taking a direct hit to the face from Haruhi's rocket of a beach ball and sinking underwater.

An hour later Koizumi and I climbed out of the water and sat by the pool with cheerful infants screaming in the background.

We were definitely out of place here. What was Haruhi thinking when she chose this public pool? I'm not saying that there had to be a waterslide, but I'm pretty sure there were more appropriate places for a group of high schoolers to go.

I could feel the blazing sunlight rapidly increasing the amount of melanin in my skin. That made me wonder if Nagato could tan, so I looked around for her and found the small, short-haired, reticent girl was sitting back in the shade, her sage eyes staring into space.

The same way she always looked. Nagato was practically a statue, no matter where we went—or so I thought.

"Hmm?"

I was hit by a sense of bafflement before it quickly vanished. There was that strange feeling again. For a moment I could feel that Nagato was bored. Déjà vu. Yeah, and then Haruhi would say the following—

"These two are my brigade members. They'll do whatever I say, so feel free to ask for anything."

I turned back to the pool to find that Haruhi had walked over to us with a group of little girls in tow.

Asahina was up to her chin in the water with her eyes closed, probably tired out from having to deal with a bunch of hyper grade-schoolers. Haruhi, who probably had fewer worries than those grade-schoolers, was in top gear as she turned her shining eyes toward Koizumi and me.

"Hey, let's go have a blast. We're gonna play underwater soccer. The two guys can be goalies."

What kind of sport is that and what kind of rules are involved? But before I could ask, that sense of déjà vu disappeared.

"...Yeah."

I gave her a perfunctory reply as we stood up. Koizumi had a smile on his face as he joined the circle of children.

That strange feeling was gone now.

Hmm. Well, it's a fairly common phenomenon. To dream about a moment from everyday life. Besides, I came to this pool when I was a kid. It's possible that a memory or two may have resurfaced. Or there was a slight malfunction in the complex process my brain used to transmit data.

I pushed aside a nearby dolphin-shaped inflatable before chasing after the beach ball Haruhi had just bicycle-kicked.

Once we had had as much fun as we could possibly stand, we left the public pool. On the way back I was one of the acrobatic trio while Koizumi enjoyed a tandem of adolescence incarnate. This is why people snap.

Asahina was sitting elegantly on the rack, her pale skin making the flush in her cheeks more pronounced as the blood rushed to her head. When I saw that one of her arms was wrapped around the waist of the rider on the saddle, I was about ready to pop a vessel. If I concentrated hard enough, I could almost hear the wind howling.

I pedaled away on the bicycle in whichever direction Haruhi pointed and eventually ended up back at our meeting place in front of the station.

Oh, that's right. I have to pay for everybody.

Once we settled down at the café, I placed a cold, wet towel on my forehead and slumped back in my seat. One second later:

"I came up with a list of activities for us to do. What do you think?"

The sheet of paper made its majestic descent to the table as Haruhi pointed for us to look at it. A letter-sized sheet of paper torn out of a notebook.

"What is this?"

Haruhi responded to my question boastfully.

"An itinerary for how we're spending what little remains of summer vacation."

"For who?"

"For us. The SOS Brigade's Summer Special Series."

Haruhi drained her glass of water and asked the server for another.

"I just noticed. We only have two weeks of summer vacation left. That left me in a state of shock. Yowzers! It feels like there are so many things I still want to do, but our time is limited. We'll be kicking it up a notch."

Haruhi's handwritten outline said the following.

STUFF WE HAVE TO DO OVER SUMMER VACATION

- Summer camp
- Pool
- Bon Dance
- Fireworks
- Part-time job
- Stargazing
- Batting practice
- Insect collecting
- Test of courage
- Etc.

Summer fever.

This disease had probably escaped from the jungle somehow. It must have been spread by mosquitoes or some equivalent. I'd have to feel sorry for any mosquito that sucked Haruhi's blood. Probably end up with food poisoning.

Of the above, "Summer camp" and "Pool" were crossed out with large X's. I guess that meant they'd been completed.

Which meant that we had to clear this list in less than two weeks? And what was that "Etc." supposed to mean? There was still more to come?

"If I think of something. For now, this is all. Is there anything else you want to do? What about Mikuru?"

"Um…"

Asahina began thinking in earnest while I tried to make eye contact and send her a message. Don't suggest anything exotic…

"I'd like to scoop goldfish."

"Okay."

Haruhi used her ballpoint pen to add another item to the list.

Haruhi proceeded to ask Nagato and Koizumi if they had any requests, but Nagato shook her head wordlessly while Koizumi declined with a light smile. The correct choice.

"Excuse me for a second."

Koizumi had quickly finished his iced café au lait and proceeded to snatch the sheet of paper and study it. He appeared to be deep in thought, as though he were trying to track something down. Did this list of events warrant that kind of behavior?

For the next few minutes I watched as Nagato sipped soda through her straw without a sound.

"Thank you."

Koizumi returned Haruhi's so-called outline to the table and tilted his head slightly. What's that supposed to mean?

"We begin tomorrow. Meet up here in front of the station again tomorrow! Is there a Bon Dance going on anywhere nearby tomorrow? Fireworks would also work."

Look this stuff up before we begin.

"I'll look into it," Koizumi volunteered. "I'll be in touch later. Just Bon Dances for now. Or the location of a fireworks festival, correct?"

"Don't forget about goldfish-scooping, Koizumi. It's a rare request from Mikuru."

"Should I search for a location that combines the Bon Dance with a festival?"

"Yep, please do. We're counting on you, Koizumi."

Haruhi was in a good mood as she gulped down the ice cream from her coffee float in one bite and folded up the sheet of notebook paper as though it were a map that led to a treasure island.

While I paid the bill, Haruhi ran off like a jogger practicing for an upcoming race. She may be trying to save her pent-up energy for tomorrow. If she's going to detonate, I would prefer her to go out with a bang instead of dragging the process out. Wouldn't have to waste time picking up the pieces that way.

The remaining four brigade members went our separate ways, and once I was sure that the other two were far enough away, I called out to the backside of the remaining one.

"Nagato."

The organic humanoid clad in a summer sailor uniform turned in response to my voice.

" . . . "

She stared back at me wordlessly with a neutral expression on her pale face—two artificial-looking eyes that showed neither rejection nor acceptance.

I was bugged by how something felt wrong. Nagato showing

no emotions was business as usual, but there was something odd about Nagato today that I couldn't quite put my finger on.

"Well…"

I managed to stop her, but now I was flustered after realizing that I didn't have anything to say.

"It's nothing, really. How have you been? Are you doing okay?"

Why am I asking pointless questions?

Nagato blinked slowly before nodding so slightly that you'd need a protractor to tell.

"Okay."

"That's good to hear."

"Yes."

Her rigid face, which barely ever showed any signs of movement, appeared to be even tighter…no, I've got it backward. It seems to have loosened up, oddly enough…I have no idea how my eyes could completely contradict themselves. I guess I'll just say that human perception is limited and leave it at that.

In the end, I couldn't find anything else to say, so I bid a hasty farewell and turned away from Nagato to make my escape.

For some reason I had a feeling that it was better this way. And so I rode my bicycle back home, ate dinner, took a shower, and watched TV before eventually falling asleep.

The next morning I was woken from my idle slumber by another call from Haruhi.

She'd found a place holding a Bon Dance festival. It'd be this evening at the public grounds.

There you have it.

Found one at the perfect time, huh? As I was appreciating this fact, Haruhi said the following.

"Let's all go buy summer kimonos."

That was how today's schedule would begin, apparently.

"Originally, I'd planned on wearing them for Tanabata, but accidentally forgot. Something must have been wrong with me. The fact that Japanese customs allow for the wearing of summer kimonos two months in a row is a real lifesaver."

Lives were saved?

I should mention that it was broad daylight. This would explain why we had to meet up so early for a nighttime event. Just like the day before, Haruhi was all on her high horse, Asahina was mellow, Nagato was silent, and Koizumi had that smirk on his face as we gathered in front of the station like clockwork.

"Mikuru and Yuki don't have summer kimonos. I don't either. I was passing through the shopping district the other day when I saw a place that sold the whole outfit, sandals and all, for a cheap price. Let's go there."

I watched Asahina and Nagato stand there as I pictured the female members in summer kimonos.

Well, it is summer.

Koizumi and I would go in our usual clothes. Save the fancy bathrobes for hotels. I sure don't want to see a man in a summer kimono.

"That's true. Koizumi would look good, but in your case?"

Haruhi snorted as she looked me up and down.

"Okay, let's go."

She delivered her order as she waved the fan in her hand.

"Off to the kimono store we go!"

Once Haruhi entered the women's clothing shop, she arbitrarily chose Asahina's and Nagato's outfits before stomping over to a changing room.

Nagato was the only one who knew how to put a summer kimono on, so the other two needed the help of a female clerk, which was very time-consuming. Koizumi and I were left to wander the racks of women's clothing until the three of them finally assembled in front of the mirrors.

Haruhi's had a flashy hibiscus pattern, Asahina's had goldfish of all colors, and Nagato's featured a bunch of plain geometric shapes. Each summer kimono was becoming in its own way, which left me confused about where to look.

The female clerk was glancing at Koizumi and me as if she wanted to know who was whose boyfriend, but too bad for her. Koizumi aside, I was just an escort. Am I supposed to feel disappointed?

Well, I got to see the summer-kimono version of Asahina, so it's all good. Haruhi and Nagato also looked good in their own ways. Not that this needed to be said out loud.

"Mikuru, you're…"

Haruhi took one look at Asahina and burst into joy.

"Absolutely adorable! I must be a genius. I knew I had the right idea! The sight of you in a summer kimono will have ninety-five percent of the men in this world fawning over you!"

I asked about the remaining five percent.

"Her charms aren't going to work on gay men. Five out of every hundred guys are gay. Never forget that."

I really doubt I'll ever need that information.

Asahina also seemed rather pleased as she spun around in front of the fitting room mirror and examined her attire.

"So this would be the traditional dress in this country. It's a bit tight across the chest, but it looks wonderful…"

This was definitely one of the better costumes Haruhi had forced on her. Didn't show as much skin as the bunny outfit, and felt less exotic than the maid uniform. A costume that was perfectly safe to wear around town this time of year. Like a natural feature of summer. And she looked damn good in it. It was almost like I was looking at my sister in a summer kimono, with the exception of the unbalanced swelling above her sash. Still, if it's cute, it's all good. There was a divine aura emitting from Asahina's entire body that made you willing to forgive anything. She could become the mastermind of a bank robbery and I would willingly plead her case. Don't know if I could say the same for Haruhi.

Since Haruhi and her lack of time management had forced us to assemble bright and early, we had a sizable amount of time left before the Bon Dance festival. Thus we had no choice but to kill time at the park in front of the station, during which time Haruhi braided Asahina's and Nagato's hair. The two of them obediently sat on the bench like dolls as Haruhi kept changing their hairstyles, each one stunning enough that I felt like snapping away with a camera, until the sun finally began to set and we lined up to head for the public grounds.

The Bon Dance festival was already bustling with activity, despite the fact that it was still light out, as people flooded in out of nowhere. I'm surprised by all the people here.

"Wow."

Asahina was unreserved in expressing her admiration.

" ... "

Nagato never reacted to anything.

I've never actually seen someone dance at a Bon Dance, and this time was no different. But a Bon Dance, huh? Haven't seen one in forever—

"Hmm?"

There it is again. A headache with a tinge of déjà vu. Pretty sure I haven't been to one in years, yet it feels like I just went to one recently. The stage in the center of the grounds and the festival stands around all seem vaguely familiar...

But then, as though I were grasping at the threads of a spiderweb dangling in the air, that sensation abruptly vanished.

I could hear Haruhi's voice.

"Mikuru, there's the goldfish scooping you wanted to do. Scoop all you want. You get an extra two hundred points for a black moor."

Haruhi made up her own rules as she took Asahina's hand and dashed over to the tank for scooping goldfish.

"Shall we join them? How about a contest to see who can catch more?"

The game-loving Koizumi made a proposal, and I immediately shook my head. I don't have a bowl to put goldfish in. Anyway, I'm more interested in the food vendors and the mouthwatering aromas of their wares.

"What about you, Nagato? Wanna grab something to eat?"

She looked at me with cheerless eyes before slowly turning away. Her eyes were focused on a mask vendor. That's what you're interested in? I really don't get her.

"Oh, well. Let's have a look around."

The speakers began playing easy-listening festival music. I took Nagato to the mask vendor, with Koizumi being a nuisance and tagging along.

"That was a fine haul, but I only took one, since I didn't need that many. Mikuru couldn't catch any, so I gave her one of mine."

There was a small plastic bag dangling from Asahina's finger that contained a very plain, small orange fish swimming without a care. The way Asahina tightly gripped the string was adorable to watch. Her other hand held a candy apple, which gave me the idea to buy one to take home for my sister. Can't hurt to get on her good side every now and then.

Meanwhile, Haruhi was toying with a yo-yo balloon in her left hand while carrying a tray of takoyaki, octopus dumplings, in her right.

"You can have one."

And with that, she extended the tray. I was savoring the taste of the takoyaki dripping with sauce when—

"Huh? Yuki, what's with the mask?"

"Bought one," Nagato said as she stared at the toothpick protruding from her takoyaki. The side of Nagato's head was adorned by a silver alien. I suppose that she probably felt connected to it in some way, as an alien herself, since she'd gone so far as to extend her paw from her sleeve to point it out.

I had a feeling that I was in Nagato's debt, so I wouldn't have had a problem with buying that for her, but Nagato had declined without a word and paid for it herself. That reminds me. What does she do for income?

The stage was surrounded by women in summer kimonos and children swaying to the sounds of traditional music. Felt like I was watching a gathering of associations for old people, women, and children. Anyone who came to a Bon Dance to have fun would never actually dance. Naturally, we weren't.

Asahina was watching the dancing people with as much fascination as if she had been watching locals do a backward jungle dance in welcome.

"Ooh— Aah—"

She softly expressed her appreciation. They don't have Bon Dances in the future?

With Haruhi leading our little band, we browsed the festival before the rest of us were eventually reduced to servants trailing after Haruhi as she pointed out foods she wanted to eat or attractions she wanted to try. Haruhi certainly appeared to be enjoying herself, and Asahina did as well, which made this fun for me. I couldn't tell if Nagato was having fun or not, and I couldn't have cared less about how Koizumi felt.

Every now and then Koizumi would suddenly fall silent before

quickly smiling again. This guy's been having mood swings of his own the past couple of days. Though that may be the fate of every person who joins the SOS Brigade.

It was summer. Summer vacation.

As I watched the three girls in their summer kimonos, I had a feeling that those words could excuse anything that might happen.

So when Haruhi said the following:

"Let's do fireworks, fireworks. We're already dressed for it. Get it out of the way today."

I was all for it. We bought a cheap fireworks package for children at one of the stands and headed off to a nearby riverbed, where the summer night sky would only be illuminated by the moon and Mars. On our way there we stopped to buy a hundred-yen lighter and an instant camera. The rest of us followed after Haruhi, who marched along while swinging her yo-yo balloon and waving her fan. She seemed to be even more hyper than usual. For some reason I was reminded of the phrase "The clothes make the (wo)man."

As I stared at Haruhi's bouncing hair I couldn't even bring myself to warn her about taking long strides in a summer kimono. Haruhi is defined by her pep and strength.

For the next hour I took numerous pictures of Asahina staring wide-eyed at a sparkler, Haruhi running around with a fountain firework in each hand, and Nagato staring at a black snake twisting and turning, before the SOS Brigade's summer activities were over for the day.

Haruhi glanced over at Koizumi, who was placing the remains of the fireworks in a plastic bag after dipping them in the river, before tracing her lips with her finger and speaking.

"We can do insect collecting tomorrow, then."

It would appear that she intended to clear off every item on her list.

"Haruhi, there's nothing wrong with having fun, but have you finished your summer homework?"

Not that I was in any position to talk when I hadn't even touched mine. Haruhi looked puzzled for a moment.

"What's wrong with you? That little bit of homework only takes three days to finish. I finished mine back in July. That's how I always do it. Get the painful stuff over with early so you're free to have fun without any worries. That would be the correct way to enjoy summer vacation."

Haruhi sincerely believed that it was only a little bit of homework. Why does a girl like her have brains? God did a pretty half-assed job of spreading the wealth.

Haruhi gave us a glare.

"Bring bug-catching nets and insect cages when we assemble. Got it? Yes. We'll have a contest to see who can collect the most. The winner gets to be brigade chief for a day!"

Who would want that title? So any insect will do?

"Well...they have to be cicadas! Yep, this will be the SOS Brigade Cicada Hunt. The rules are...any type will do. Whoever catches the most wins!"

Haruhi was making decisions and getting excited by herself as she swung her fan around as though she were trying to catch an insect. Net and cage, huh? Think I have those in my closet. From a long time ago.

And when I finally made it back home, I realized that I'd forgotten to buy a candy apple for my sister.

The next day there wasn't a single cloud in sight, despite the fact that I'd driven a long nail into one of those rainmaking dolls in the hopes that it would pour. The cicadas seemed quite pleased with the hottest summer day so far.

"I wonder if cicadas are edible. They might taste good if we deep-fry them. You know, I've been wondering. Does deep-fried stuff taste good because of the batter? If that's the case, cicadas would work."

Eat them by yourself.

Don't you find anything wrong with the sight of a group of five high schoolers carrying nets and cages?

We assembled before noon and made our way toward North High in search of greenery. After all, our high school was in the middle of the mountains, so there were more than enough trees around, and forests were the ideal habitat for insects. I had believed that I lived in a fairly big city, but apparently it wasn't as barren as I thought.

The area was swarming with crying bugs, as if every tree trunk were covered by cicadas. Plenty for everyone. Even Asahina, stumbling around while flailing with her net, was able to catch a few. The cicadas here apparently fail to recognize that humans are the greatest danger to their existence. Now would be a good time to tell them.

After catching numerous cicadas, I watched as they sat still in the cage. I have no idea how many years they'd spent underground, but I'm pretty sure that they didn't molt so Haruhi could fry them. Besides, I'd been feeling a little guilty about the decrease in crying insects during the past few summers. Sorry about spreading asphalt everywhere. Please forgive human ignorance.

Haruhi couldn't possibly have heard my monologue, but nevertheless, she said the following.

"You need to follow the spirit of catch and release. If we let them go, they might return the favor in the future."

I imagined a human-size cicada knocking on the door to my house. If somebody were to come back and return the favor after being arbitrarily caught and released, he'd be as dumb as a bug. Revenge would make more sense.

Haruhi opened her insect cage and shook it back and forth.

"There! Go back to the mountains!"

Bzzz—A number of cicadas bumped against one another before flying out of the cage and soaring over Asahina, who let out an adorable shriek as she crouched down, and right past the head of Nagato, standing perfectly still, before disappearing into the sunset in spirals and straight lines.

I followed suit. As I watched the cicadas pour out, I almost felt like I was Pandora accidentally opening the box from Hermes. It didn't occur to me to keep one for myself until the cicadas were all long gone out of sight.

On the next day, there was employment waiting for us.

Haruhi was kind enough to share this part-time job she'd managed to find. Our work for the day consisted of:

"W-welcome—" I could hear Asahina stuttering hesitantly.

"Okay, everybody line up. Ah, ah…don't push."

The job that Haruhi had strong-armed us into like a pushy salesman was to bring in customers at a local supermarket's grand opening sale.

We were assembled without knowing what was going on, stuffed into costumes without knowing what was going on, and forced to promote the supermarket starting at ten in the morning.

I should mention that these were animal mascot costumes.

Seriously, I don't get it. Why do I have to wear this thing? Isn't it Asahina's job to wear different costumes…? Hey, Koizumi and Nagato! You should also complain! Why are you following her orders in silence?

"Please line up. I'm begging you!"

I could hear Asahina, clad in green, stumble over her words as I sweat like a pig.

We were dressed as frogs. And our job was to hand children

balloons. Apparently this was a special event that was part of the annual celebration to commemorate the original grand opening. Any customers who brought their families would receive free balloons.

Only kids could ever get excited over a little freebie like this. Hey, brat with the stupid look on your face. I'll give you this red balloon. There you go.

Asahina the tree frog was especially popular. Incidentally, Koizumi was a black-spotted pond frog and I was a toad. We didn't have any choice. Nagato, dressed as a Surinam horned frog, used the pump to inflate balloons for the three of us to pass out while Haruhi stayed cool indoors in her regular clothes. There's gonna be mutiny if she's paid the same as the rest of us.

Apparently the owner of the store was an acquaintance of Haruhi's. He'd smiled when Haruhi walked up to him and said, "Hey, old-timer."

After two hours of hard work, the balloons ran out and everybody besides Haruhi headed to a storeroom-like area to remove the excess garments. Now I know how it feels for a snake to shed its skin. I've rarely ever felt so relieved the past few years.

Nagato walked out with an aloof expression, but Asahina, Koizumi, and I were dripping with sweat as we slid out of the frog suits and remained silent for a while.

"Whew—"

I no longer had the energy to carefully observe Asahina in her flimsy tank top and short skirt.

"Good work."

When Haruhi showed up eating ice cream, I seriously wanted to bury her up to her neck in a hot desert.

And as a finishing blow, our pay came in the form of that tree frog costume. Based on Haruhi's nonchalant revelation, this had been her goal from the very beginning. She held the thin discarded green frog disguise under her arm as though she were a general who had just been awarded one hundred pounds of gold. Our well-deserved pay never existed to begin with.

"What's wrong with that? I've wanted this for a long time. My wish has been granted. The old-timer said he'd give it to me for Mikuru's sake. Mikuru, I'll award you a special handmade medal. I haven't made it yet though, so hang on."

One more piece of garbage to add to Asahina's belongings. It'll probably be an armband with the word "medal" written on it.

But.

"I'll stick this frog in the clubroom as a souvenir. Mikuru, feel free to wear this whenever you want. I give you permission!"

I couldn't bring myself to feel angry after seeing the look on Haruhi's face.

I was completely exhausted. After constant activity day and night between the pool, insect collecting, and sauna à la giant costume, any perfectly healthy high school boy would be on his last legs.

Thus I was sound asleep that night in a tranquil dreamland until my cell phone began to ring.

Nothing pisses me off more than being woken up in the middle of the night by a pointless phone call. It's an unreasonable time to call other people, and Haruhi was the only person I knew who was irrational enough to do such a thing, so I was fully prepared to yell at her as I pressed the Talk button on my cell phone half-asleep, only to hear, "…Moan (sniff)…groan (sob)…"

The sound of a girl crying. It sent shivers down my spine. I instantly woke up. This is bad. I just heard something I wasn't supposed to.

A second before I was about to toss the phone down—

"Kyon…"

I was able to recognize Asahina's voice through the sobbing.

"Hello, Asahina?"

Don't tell me that she's calling to say good-bye forever. This better not be anything like the famous folktale of Princess Kaguya going back to the moon. I realized that the "present time" was only a temporary residence for her. I understood that she would eventually have to return to the future. Had the time come? I won't accept a farewell over the phone.

However, the lovely lady on the other end of the phone continued.

"I…ah, something terrible has…*sob*…*hic*…at this rate…I, waahhh…"

She was making about as much sense as a grade-schooler with her words all slurred together. I was wondering what I was supposed to do when—

"Why hello. This is Koizumi."

The cheerful voice of a damn man took over.

What? Why are they together at this late hour? Why am I not there? Your head will be separated from your body in five seconds, Koizumi, if you don't appease me with an answer I can accept.

"We have a bit of a situation on our hands. A particularly difficult one, which was why Asahina contacted me."

Before contacting me? I'm not very happy about that.

"There wouldn't have been any point in consulting you…no, excuse me. In fact, I was also unable to provide any help. A perilous predicament."

I scratched my head furiously.

"Is Haruhi on the verge of ending the world again?"

"Technically, no. In fact, it would be the exact opposite. As things stand at the moment, the world can never end."

Huh? Am I still dreaming? What is this guy talking about?

Koizumi sensed my confusion and continued.

"I already contacted Nagato. As expected, she was already aware of the situation. The details will become clear if we ask Nagato. Which is why I must ask, would it be possible for us to meet up right now? Minus Suzumiya, naturally."

Of course it'd be possible. Any person capable of abandoning a weeping Asahina would deserve to be sliced up seven times and more.

"I'll be right there. Where are you?"

Koizumi told me his location. In front of the usual station. The SOS Brigade's official meeting place.

And so I got changed, sneaked through the hallway of my house, and took off on my bicycle to find three shadowy figures waiting upon my arrival. The streets weren't completely deserted, as I'd spotted a few students here and there. As a result, we were able to blend in with the crowd of fools with nowhere to go on a summer night and conduct our dubious meeting without any worries. Though I was definitely starting to nod off.

Asahina, dressed in pastels, was crouching in front of the station with a disheveled Koizumi and Nagato in a sailor uniform flanking her like a pair of decorative pine trees. Asahina must have thrown on whatever was handy because her clothes didn't match at all. She must have been in a real panic or pressed for time.

The tallest of them apparently noticed me, as he waved me over.

"So what's going on?"

The faint glow from the lamppost illuminated the soft expression on Koizumi's face.

"I apologize for calling you out at such a late hour. However, Asahina is rather distraught, as you can see."

Asahina was squatting down and sobbing like a melting snowman. She looked up at me with a tearful face and dry eyes. Eyes so captivating that I was on the verge of throwing away everything to help her out.

"Wah, Kyon, I…" Asahina sniffed before murmuring to herself.

"I can no longer return to the future…"

"Allow me to summarize. Basically, we are stuck in an infinite time loop."

Hard to believe something so ludicrous when you have a smile on your face. Did Koizumi have any idea what he was saying?

"Of course. I am fully aware of the implications. I was discussing the matter with Asahina earlier."

Call me. So I can be part of that discussion.

"As a result, we realized that something was odd about the recent flow of time. You should credit the discovery to Asahina. She was able to confirm my suspicion."

What suspicion?

"That we are experiencing the same period of time over and over."

I've already heard about that.

"To be precise, it would be the period from August seventeenth to the thirty-first."

Koizumi's words sounded rather hollow to me.

"We are currently in the middle of a summer vacation with no end."

"We're certainly on summer vacation right now."

"A literally endless summer. In this world we will never see September, much less autumn. There is no future after August. That is why Asahina cannot return to the future. It all makes sense. It's only natural that she cannot communicate with the future when the future no longer exists."

How could the physical lack of a future be natural? Time marches on, regardless of what we do. I stared at the top of Asahina's head as I spoke.

"Who would ever believe that?"

"I was hoping that you might believe me, since I couldn't possibly tell Suzumiya."

Koizumi also looked down at Asahina.

I should mention that Asahina at least tried to explain. To the accompaniment of intermittent sobs.

"*Sniff*, um...I normally use <classified information> to contact the future...*sniff*. But after a week without <classified information>, I was starting to wonder if something was wrong. And then <classified information>...I was so surprised that I tried to <classified information> in a rush, but there wasn't any <classified information>...*sob*. *Hic*. What do I do...?"

I have no idea what you should do, but does that <classified information> work like some kind of censor?

"Are we trapped in some kind of weird world created by Haruhi? Like a real-life version of that closed space thing?"

Koizumi had his arms crossed as he leaned against the vending machine and rejected my hypothesis in a light tone.

"The world has not been recreated. Suzumiya has cut off a sector of time. The period from August seventeenth to the thirty-first. Thus, we are currently in a world that only consists of two weeks. Any point before August seventeenth or after August thirty-first has disappeared. This is a world that will never see September."

He exhaled in what sounded like a failed attempt to whistle.

"There is a process right before midnight on August thirty-first where everything is reset and returned to the seventeenth."

What about our...I mean, everybody's memories?

"Those are also reset, as if the two weeks leading up to that point never happened. Everybody starts over from the beginning."

Somebody must really love to screw with time. Though I suppose I shouldn't be surprised when there's a time traveler among us.

"No, Asahina has nothing to do with this incident. The situation is not as simple as you have deemed."

How do you know?

"Only Suzumiya would be capable of such a feat. Or did you have somebody else in mind?"

You'd have to be delusional or a chronic daydreamer to have a list of potential psychopaths on hand.

"What am I supposed to do?"

"The matter will be as good as solved when we figure that out."

Koizumi appeared to be enjoying himself. He certainly didn't seem to be very worried. Why?

"I finally know the source of the strange sensation I've been experiencing the past few days."

Koizumi revealed the reason why.

"You must have felt the same way. Starting from the day we went to the public pool, there have been intermittent, intense flashes of déjà vu. In retrospect, I would say that they were remnants of the memories from previous loops—for lack of a better way to describe it. We were sensing the parts left over from the reset."

Could the whole world be feeling the same way?

"I doubt that. You and I are the exceptions. People who are close to Suzumiya appear to have a higher chance of noticing the anomaly."

"What about Haruhi? Is she aware of what's going on?"

"It seems that she's utterly clueless. Though you could say that it's better this way…"

Koizumi gave Nagato a sideways glance before casually posing a question.

"So then, how many times have we repeated the last two weeks of August?"

Nagato answered with a calm expression on her face.

*   *   *

"This would be the fifteen thousand four hundred ninety-eighth incarnation."

I felt faint for a moment there.

Fifteen thousand four hundred ninety-eight. That's over thirty characters written out, while 15,498 feels considerably smaller. Yay for Arabic numerals. I feel like offering a prayer of thanks to whoever it was who came up with the idea. This derailment only serves to show how disturbed I was.

"We have repeated the same two weeks over ten thousand times. If an ordinary person were to be aware of this loop and retain the memories from each incarnation, he would experience a mental breakdown. I believe that Suzumiya's memories have been completely wiped clean, cleaner than ours," Koizumi explained.

This is when you turn to the most knowledgeable person around. I checked with Nagato.

"Are you serious about this?"

"Yes."

Nagato nodded.

So wait, we've already done the stuff scheduled for tomorrow in the past? Along with the Bon Dance and goldfish scooping?

"That is not necessarily the case."

Nagato's voice wasn't showing much emotion either.

"Haruhi Suzumiya has not followed the same course of action in each of the previous fifteen thousand four hundred ninety-seven incarnations."

Nagato gave me an unconcerned look as she spoke in that unconcerned tone.

"Over the course of the previous fifteen thousand four hundred ninety-seven loops, there were two instances without a trip to the Bon Dance. There were four hundred and thirty-seven instances where the trip occurred without goldfish scooping. At the moment, every loop has included a visit to the public pool. There were nine thousand twenty-five instances of working part-time, but there have been six different variations. Aside from distributing balloons, we have also been carrying objects, manning cash registers, passing out flyers, working a call center, and modeling for a photo shoot. Of those, there were six thousand eleven instances of balloon distribution and three hundred sixty instances of two or more jobs performed. The incarnations with multiple jobs can be divided into—"

"Yeah, that's enough."

I silenced the alien-made artificial human before putting my thinking cap on.

We'd been through the back half of August fifteen thousand four—oh screw it—15,498 times. Everything was reset on August thirty-first, and we started over from August seventeenth. I had no recollection of this happening, but Nagato did—why?

"Because Nagato, or the Data Overmind, to be precise, is an existence that transcends space-time."

Koizumi's smug smirk seemed a bit forced, or maybe it was just the light.

Or whatever, doesn't matter. Moving on. I understand that Nagato and her boss are capable of such a feat. But that wasn't my concern. This all meant that...

"So, Nagato. You've actually experienced this two-week period fifteen thousand four hundred ninety-seven times?"

"Yes."

Nagato nodded like it wasn't a big deal. Yes? Don't you have anything else to say? Not that *I* can think of anything else to say. But still...

"Well, you see..."

Hold on. Fifteen thousand four hundred ninety-eight times. Multiplied by two weeks. That comes out to 216,972 days. Uh, around 594 years. She's gone through centuries, loop after loop, just standing there and watching us impassively? How could anyone not be sick and tired of that? I mean, after 15,498 visits to the public pool?

"Man…"

My mouth remained open as my voice trailed off. Nagato cocked her head like a small bird as she stared at me.

I recalled that feeling I'd had when I saw Nagato sitting by the pool. Guess I might have been correct when I thought that she looked bored. I'd assume that even Nagato would get sick of all that repetition. She never says anything, but she might have clicked her tongue or something while no one was looking—and that was when a sudden thought hit me. I more or less understood the phenomenon we were dealing with, but I didn't know why this was happening.

"Why is Haruhi doing this?"

"This is merely speculation."

Koizumi gave a little disclaimer.

"Suzumiya doesn't want summer vacation to end on a subconscious level. That is why our summer vacation won't end."

Because she's acting like a little brat who doesn't want to go back to school?

Koizumi absently traced his finger around the rim of his can of coffee.

"I would presume that she feels there still is something left to be done during summer vacation. She can't begin the new term until that's been done, or else she'll have lingering regrets. And when she falls asleep on the night of August thirty-first with that gnawing regret…"

She wakes up to find that the clock has been turned back two weeks. Yeah, I'm just about ready to give up on her. I knew she was capable of doing just about anything, but this takes her lack of common sense to a whole new level.

"What will it take to satisfy her?"

"I haven't the slightest. Do you know, Nagato?"

"I do not."

Didn't take her long to respond. You realize you're the only one we can depend on here. I attempted to voice that thought.

"Why didn't you tell us? That we've been engaged in an endless two-week-long waltz."

After a few seconds of silence, Nagato's thin lips parted.

"My job is to observe."

"...I see."

I already knew that, more or less. Nagato had yet to actively involve herself in any of our activities. But she got involved, in the end, almost every time. However, she's only initiated contact once, when she invited me to her apartment. Barring that exception, Nagato's merely accompanied us in her extremely vital position.

How could I forget? Yuki Nagato was a humanoid interface created by the Data Overmind. An organic android dispatched to observe Haruhi. There might be a safety mechanism on her ability to feel emotion.

"But none of that matters."

What mattered was that I considered Yuki Nagato, the book-loving, reticent, petite, and ever-so-reliable classmate, one of us.

If you looked at the SOS Brigade members, Nagato had the most knowledge as well as the ability to apply that knowledge. So I had a few more questions for her.

"When did we first realize this?"

I asked this question on a whim, but Nagato answered as though she'd been expecting it.

"The eight thousand seven hundred sixty-ninth loop. Revelation has become more frequent as of late."

"Since we are consistently finding ourselves disoriented by déjà vu."

Koizumi seemed to agree.

"However, during those past sequences, we were unable to correct the flow of time after realizing our situation."

"Yes," said Nagato.

Which explained why Asahina was crying right now. Because she now knew the truth. And then, two weeks' worth of memories, experience, and growth would be reset…and she'd find herself crying after learning the truth again.

And once again, I find myself with the same reaction I've had more times than I care to remember since meeting Haruhi back in spring. The same reaction I've had every time Haruhi created some kind of godforsaken mess. The same reaction I have right now.

What the hell.

And I've had that reaction 8,769 times in the past two weeks.

Seriously…

Chalk up another ridiculous conversation.

We went stargazing the next day.

The location was the roof of Nagato's apartment. Koizumi brought a bulky telescope that he mounted on a tripod. It was around eight PM.

The sky was dark, and so was Asahina's mood. She just stood there in a dazed stupor. This really wasn't the time to be looking at the stars. I wasn't in much better shape myself.

Koizumi, who seemed to have recovered his composure, busied himself with setting up the telescope with a smile on his face.

"This was a hobby of mine when I was young. I was deeply moved when I saw the moons of Jupiter for the first time."

Nagato was the same as always, just standing there on the roof.

I looked up at the night sky, but there were only a handful of stars. The polluted air made them difficult to see. You could even say that there was no sky to see. Come winter, the atmosphere would clear and Orion would be visible, at the very least.

The telescope was pointed at Earth's neighbor. Haruhi was peering through the finder.

"I wonder if any exist."

"Any what?"

"Martians."

I'd rather they didn't. I pictured a bunch of octopus-like monsters wriggling around as they plotted world domination, and it certainly didn't sound entertaining in the slightest.

"Why? They could be a friendly bunch. Look, there's nobody on the surface. I'm sure they're just a really reserved race who live in underground caverns. They're trying to avoid scaring us Earthlings."

The Martians in Haruhi's head sound like residents of Hollow Earth. Can't you make up your mind? Are we talking Pellucidar or *Mars Attacks!*? You'll only make things more complicated if you combine them. Think simple, simple.

"I'm sure they have a plan to pop out and welcome us when the first manned spacecraft lands on Mars. They'll be like, 'Welcome to Mars, neighbors, denizens of our neighboring planet!' I'm sure of it."

That'd be a bigger scare. Practically an ambush. I have no idea who's going to be the first to step on Martian soil, but we should probably warn that person. Do I address the letter to NASA?

Time passed as we took turns using the telescope to observe the patterns of Mars and lunar craters. I suddenly noticed that someone was missing and began glancing around before I found Asahina sitting against the rooftop railing and hugging her knees. She had her head bowed down and her eyes were shut. Doubt she got much sleep last night, so I'll let her rest for now.

Haruhi had apparently grown tired of a night sky that showed no signs of dramatic change.

"Let's look for UFOs. They're probably targeting Earth. There must be alien scouts standing by in orbit."

She cheerfully began turning the telescope this way and that but soon lost interest again. She sat down next to Asahina and leaned against her slender shoulder before falling asleep.

Koizumi turned to me and spoke in a soft voice.

"She must have worn herself out."

"I don't see how she would be more tired than the rest of us."

Haruhi was sound asleep. I was tempted to draw on her face. Still, she looked her best when she was asleep, yeah? If only she would keep her mouth shut. If she swapped personalities with Nagato, that would be perfect. Well, a subdued Haruhi is one thing, but I can't even begin to imagine a talkative Nagato whose moods swing all over the place.

A night breeze blew by as I watched Haruhi and Asahina sleeping side by side. Haruhi wasn't surrendering anything to Asahina in terms of looks at the moment. Some might even rank her above. I guarantee it.

"What does she want to do?"

I sighed to myself.

"Have fun with her friends? Something like that."

"I would assume that is the case. And we would be the friends you mentioned."

Koizumi looked off into the night sky.

"So then, which fun activity are we supposed to engage in? This won't end until we figure that out. We will be forced to repeat this two-week period until we determine what Suzumiya desires, which she herself does not know, and grant her wish. I suppose we should be grateful that our memories are being reset. Or else we would have suffered mental breakdowns long ago."

Fifteen thousand four hundred ninety-eight times.

Seriously? Isn't Nagato just trying to fool us? Quite frankly, I find

this hard to believe. Still, I could certainly see Haruhi doing something like this, since I've seen her power, still an unsolved mystery, do some blockheaded things without her knowing. Doesn't matter if she's doing something consciously or unconsciously. The end result can only mean trouble for everybody else.

And since we continue to faithfully stick with Haruhi, you have to wonder if we're some kind of overly nice goodwill organization. The SOS Brigade has some really good-tempered members. Though you know that the world's gone off its rocker when I have a say in its fate.

Besides, people like to assume that the world should be a certain way to which we absolutely must adhere, but in reality, that's just a bunch of bull that ends up tailored to different ideologies. And since they don't realize this, we find ourselves with people who blindly force their own ideals on other people. You might want to consider how future generations will view your actions in a thousand years or so.

I was going off on a nice little tangent when Koizumi suddenly interrupted me.

"I don't know what Suzumiya's looking for, but why don't we try this? Embrace her from behind without warning and whisper, 'I love you' into her ear."

"Who's supposed to do that?"

"Would anyone be more suited for the role than you?"

"I'm vetoing that idea. I pass."

"Shall I give it a try instead?"

I had no way of seeing the look on my face at that moment, since I didn't have a mirror handy. However, Koizumi could.

"I merely jest. I wouldn't be able to fulfill the role. It would only serve to confuse Suzumiya."

And with that, he began to chuckle in a grating tone.

I fell silent again as I stared up at the radiant moon, the only visible light in a hazy summer sky.

The silver disk, surrounded by engulfing darkness, almost seemed to beckon to me as it reflected brilliant sunlight. Beckon me where? Who knows?

That was all I could think about as I watched Nagato stand perfectly still and look up into the sky.

Summer wasn't quite over yet, but our summer vacation was about to end. And yet, we couldn't be entirely sure if it would ever end. Give me a break—seriously.

We might find ourselves going back to August seventeenth. How are we supposed to figure out what's still "left to be done" in Haruhi's mind?

What's left? I haven't touched the stack of homework that I'm supposed to do over summer vacation, but that shouldn't have anything to do with Haruhi. Hell, she already finished her homework.

"Where are we headed next?"

"Let's go to the batting center."

Haruhi was carrying an aluminum bat. The same beat-up bat she'd swiped from the baseball team way back when. The really old-looking one that seemed more suited for beating people to death than for hitting baseballs. Didn't realize she still had it.

Our brigade chief tossed back her hair as she flashed a million-dollar smile at all of us and led us to the batting center along the railroad tracks. I'm guessing that the inspiration for this came from watching high school baseball.

I'm also guessing that the brigade members are taking turns being melancholic. Right now we have Asahina, who's either blue or looking blue. Bad news for me, unfortunately. Guess she still wants to return to her original time.

Nagato and Koizumi were more or less back to their usual selves, Noh-mask girl and smiley-face boy, as they walked behind me.

They're acting like this isn't any of their responsibility. Could you at least pretend to look serious?

"Sigh."

I exhaled and focused my eyes ahead on Haruhi's black hair as it bounced around.

Ever since I met her, ever since the SOS Brigade was formed, someone had decided that it would be my job to babysit Haruhi. No idea who it was, so I'll have to control my urge to vent, but let me say this at least.

Don't overestimate me. I'm just your typical average Joe.

Hollow words at this point.

Asahina was a confused mess. Koizumi only ever smiled. Nagato only ever observed.

So I had to do something about Haruhi.

But what was I supposed to do?

Only Haruhi would know the answer, but she didn't even realize there was a problem.

"Mikuru, you don't need to swing the bat! Practice bunting. It's not like you're going to hit the ball if you swing. You want the ball to roll on the ground after it hits the bat. Ah, don't pop it up!"

I guess that baseball tournament had left a lasting impression on Haruhi. Don't tell me that she plans on entering again next year.

Haruhi was hogging the eighty-mph batting cage as she hit one fastball after another. She seemed to be enjoying herself so much that I found myself cheering up. This girl is really something. She must have a higher mitochondrial count than your average person. Wonder where all her energy comes from. If only she would use it for the greater good.

After that, Haruhi moved through her schedule so fast that nobody had time to hit the Pause button, as we were constantly on the move every day.

We even went to see a full-blown fireworks display. Aerial shells launched down by the shore. The three girls got back in their summer kimonos to be delighted (only Haruhi was delighted) by fireworks soaring into the sky before bursting into a fiery bloom, and to laugh at the failed attempts at making caricatures out of fireworks. Haruhi really enjoyed anything that was unnecessarily flashy. She had such an innocent smile when she was having a good time, and it made her look younger than her actual age, so I found myself averting my eyes. If I stare at her too long, I might get some weird ideas. Well, not that I know what those weird ideas might be. Still, I did understand the importance of dressing for the occasion.

On a different day we entered an open goby fishing contest on a river near the district border. We didn't catch a single goby—we kept reeling in these tiny fish that I'd never seen before—so we weren't able to participate in the measuring. Haruhi seemed to be interested in the casting motion itself, so we didn't have to deal with drastic penalties for losing or ego battles. I was very relieved and grateful that I didn't have to worry about anyone's accidentally fishing up a coelacanth, leaving me to savor the lunch that had been made by Asahina, who had turned pale upon seeing the worms used for bait and run off into the distance.

By this point Haruhi and I were burned to a crisp, in sharp contrast with Koizumi and Asahina, who had used UV protection. Nagato could probably stand there for days without tanning, which was fine with me, since a brown Nagato would be a surreal sight.

And yes, I realized that this wasn't the time to be enjoying myself.

The days flashed by as we raced along our set path.

Haruhi was full of energy. I was greatly distressed. Asahina had turned a deeper shade of blue. Koizumi's forced smile showed that he had resigned himself to this fate. Nagato was the only one who hadn't changed.

In retrospect, we did a lot of stuff over the past two weeks.

We were approaching the time limit. Today was August thirtieth. Tomorrow would be our last day of summer vacation. I had to do something today or tomorrow, but I had no idea what to do. Summer sun, chirping cicadas—everything related to summer was a source of anxiety. And a high school baseball team had been crowned champion while I wasn't paying attention. Wish this could all last a little longer.

Until Haruhi was finally satisfied.

Haruhi used the pen in her hand to cross off the items on her list.

Yesterday we waited till the dead of night to head to a large cemetery with candles in hand for our last recreational event, a test of courage. There weren't any ghosts popping out to greet us or disembodied souls floating around. The only notable highlight was Asahina whimpering timidly in vain.

"We've finished our list."

It was August thirty-first, a little past noon. We were at the usual café in front of the station.

Haruhi was staring at her sheet of paper as if the location of the lost treasures of Tokugawa were written on there in pen. Her expression was a mixture of satisfaction and regret. Under normal circumstances I would have felt a similar regret, since we had only one day of summer vacation left. Under normal circumstances.

I was seriously doubting that summer vacation would actually end. Only natural for me to be skeptical. I'd have to be, after spending months in the SOS Brigade, a ridiculous organization led by an emotionally unstable brigade chief. Makes me wish I were more shallow. Able to assume the simple mind-set that it's all good if Asahina is around... well, I'll stop there. It's possible to have too much of a good thing (the key is to use lingo that isn't necessarily applicable).

"Hmm. Was this enough?"

Haruhi seemed to be wavering as she used her straw to poke at the vanilla ice cream in her cola float.

"But yeah. I guess that's all there is. Is there anything else you want to do?"

Nagato made no response as she stared at the lemon slice in her black tea. Asahina had her fists clenched tightly above her knees, looking like a puppy that was being scolded. Koizumi merely smiled as he lifted his cup of Vienna coffee to his lips.

As for me, I couldn't think of anything to say, so I just sat there sullenly with my arms crossed as I tried to come up with something.

"Oh, well. We managed to get a lot of stuff done this summer. We visited a bunch of places, got to wear summer kimonos, and caught lots of cicadas too."

It sounded to me like Haruhi was trying to convince herself that we'd done enough. That's not the case here. It's not enough. Deep down, Haruhi doesn't want summer vacation to end yet. She may say it, but that won't change how she feels on the inside. 'Cause if we dig deep down, way deep down there, she isn't satisfied yet.

"I guess that's"—Haruhi handed me the bill—"all for today. I had tomorrow set aside in case, but you can just rest at home. I'll see you all in the clubroom in two days, then."

Haruhi stood up and moved away from the table as I started to panic.

I couldn't let Haruhi leave. That would solve nothing. The two-week repetition, discovered by Koizumi and confirmed by Nagato, will enter its 15,499th iteration.

But what was I supposed to do?

Haruhi was walking away in slow motion.

That was when, out of the blue with no warning at all—
It hit me.

A completely jumbled-up "Wait, I've seen this happen before…" kind of thing. However, this comes with a sense of vertigo like none before. An overpowering sensation of déjà vu that's stronger than anything else so far. I recognize this. Memories from the ten-thousand-plus times we've repeated this scene. August thirty-first. One day left.

There should have been some kind of hint in what Haruhi said. What was it, what was it, what was it?

"Is something wrong?"

Someone was talking. Koizumi must have mentioned something as well. Something I was worried about that I kept putting off…

Haruhi was ready to leave the way she's done thousands of times. I can't let her leave. Nothing will change. What methods have I tried before? Memories began flashing before my eyes. Everything our predecessors had tried…

And—everything they hadn't tried.

No time to think. Say something. Make a wild guess.

"My list isn't finished yet!"

I didn't need to make a big deal about it, though. Looking back later after I had calmed down, this was the creation of another memory that needed to be erased from my hippocampus. The surrounding patrons and employees, along with Haruhi, turning around from her position in front of the automatic door, focused their attention on me.

Words came pouring out on their own.

"That's right, my homework!"

Every person in the café was frozen by my sudden outburst.

"What are you talking about?"

Haruhi walked over while looking at me like I was crazy.

"Your list? Homework?"

"I haven't touched my summer homework. I have to finish that before my summer can end."

"Are you insane?"

The look she gave me implied that she thought I was. Don't care right now.

"Hey, Koizumi!"

"Yes, what is it?"

Koizumi also appeared to be taken aback.

"Did you finish yours?"

"No, we've been so busy that I'm only halfway through."

"Then we can do this together. Nagato, you too. You aren't done yet, right?"

I didn't give Nagato a chance to respond as I turned to Asahina, whose mouth was hanging open like a puppet's.

"While we're at it, I would also like Asahina to come. We're going to finish our summer list."

"Huh…?"

Asahina was a second-year, so her homework was different from ours, but that really didn't matter right now.

"B-but, um, where?"

"We can do this at my house. Bring all your notes and problem sets so we can get them all done. Nagato and Koizumi, let me copy what you have done."

Koizumi nodded.

"Is that all right with you, Nagato?"

"Yes."

The head with a pseudo–bob cut nodded slowly before looking up at me.

"Okay. Tomorrow, then. We start tomorrow morning. We'll make it happen in a single day!"

I pumped my fist in the air.

"Hold it right there!"

Haruhi had her hands on her hips as she stood next to our table. "Don't decide everything on your own. I'm the brigade chief. You're supposed to ask for my opinion first! Kyon, it's a serious violation of regulations for a brigade member to make an independent decision!"

And with that, Haruhi gave me a glare before shouting at the top of her lungs.

"I'm coming too!"

—The next day, the next morning.

Looks like I guessed right. I woke up in my own bed to find that the ordeal was over.

Because I could remember…That I had returned from the countryside after the Bon Festival. Going to the pool, catching cicadas, and all the other August memories involving Haruhi and everybody else. And best of all, I even remembered what yesterday's date was.

Yesterday was August thirty-first, and today was September first.

According to my newest memories, there had been an SOS Brigade study session in my room on the last day of summer vacation. I recall being completely exhausted. When you consider the amount of effort it took to copy all the notes in one day, I can't even imagine how much effort it would have taken to do the work on my own. I can guarantee that my vitality, energy, and spirit gauges were so low when I fell asleep last night that a single little punch would have taken me out.

Yesterday Haruhi came up to my room carrying the mountain of homework she had already finished, gave a look of disdain to Koizumi, Nagato, Asahina, and me, scribbling away with our pencils, and ended up playing with my sister the whole time.

"Don't copy word for word."

Haruhi was playing video games with my sister in the room, and she continued talking while jamming away at the controller.

"Like reword stuff and tweak calculations. The teachers aren't a bunch of idiots. Yoshizaki, the math teacher, is especially tricky. He pays extra attention to those things. Though in my opinion his own solutions aren't very elegant."

My room already felt cramped with five people plus my sister, and then my mother kept coming in with juice or lunch or snacks to make it feel even more crowded, but Haruhi, unlike the rest of us, who were engaging in so much wrist movement that carpal tunnel was imminent, appeared to be having a pretty good time. She had such a relaxed smile on her face. The smile you see higher-ups flash at lesser beings. In fact, Haruhi was so relaxed that she started giving Asahina, who was a grade above her, pointers on the essay she was struggling with. If Asahina gets a C on her report it'll be Haruhi's fault....

And with those memories firmly lodged in my mind, I got out of bed.

Today was the beginning of a new term. I think.

I've never been so glad to see the second term begin.

After the principal's speech in the gym and a shortened homeroom session, school was over. The current date was September first. I knew this because Taniguchi and Kunikida gave me such condescending looks when I asked them for the date when we were in the classroom.

The vendors and cafeteria weren't open today, so Haruhi had gone off to the snack shop outside the school gate. Koizumi and I were the only ones in the clubroom.

"Suzumiya excels both academically and athletically. I would assume that's been the case since she was a child. Which was why she didn't consider our summer homework to be a burden at all. And there was no chance that she would ever think to share the workload with friends. Since Suzumiya is fully capable of finishing the work by herself."

As I listened to Koizumi's explanation, I drew a metal chair next to the window and looked down at the schoolyard. Today was the first day of a new term, so I could have just gone home, but somehow, I ended up coming here and found myself joined by Koizumi. The most unusual thing was the absence of Nagato. She didn't let it show, but she may have been tired.

There'd been a shift in the local cicada populace from *Graptopsaltria nigrofuscata* to *Meimuna opalifera*. Summer vacation was over. That much was certain. However—

"Hard to believe it was real. That we experienced the second half of August fifteen thousand–plus times."

"It's only natural to feel that way."

Koizumi flashed a cheerful smile as he cut the deck.

"At this point we don't share any memories with the incarnations from the fifteen thousand four hundred ninety-seven other loops. They do not exist on this time axis. For we, the members of the fifteen thousand four hundred ninety-eighth time, were the only ones able to return to the normal flow of time."

However, I had been given hints. The repeated sensations of déjà vu, especially the ones at the end, may have been gifts from our predecessors. Should I even consider them predecessors, since time was more or less a merry-go-round, like those tigers that ran in circles until they turned into butter.

Still, I am here right now because of the ones who underwent those two weeks before us. I have to look at it that way or their summers, erased by Haruhi, would have been for nothing.

Especially the 8,769 incarnations who knew they were being reset.

"How about some poker?"

Koizumi was shuffling cards like a novice magician. Guess I might as well humor him.

"Sure. What are we playing for? Don't have any money on me."

"No betting, then."

And naturally, when it didn't count, I scored an insane win. The first time I've ever seen a royal flush.

If I ever get an opportunity to redo this day, I'll remember to place a bet.

PREFACE · AUTUMN

The cultural festival was over, and I found myself in a state of despondence as we entered the tail end of November.

Director Haruhi had been pretty out of control during the filming, but the movie itself performed well enough at the screening. So I figured she would be satisfied and behave herself for the time being, but there was no change in her energy level before, during, or after the cultural festival.

However, our school didn't provide enough activities to keep the wheels in Haruhi's mind spinning on a regular basis. The only event that had come up since was the election for student council president. To be honest, I was getting nervous about Haruhi's decision to run for the office, but it appeared that Haruhi had formed the odd impression that the student council was the sworn enemy of minor student associations, so she wasn't interested in infiltrating their organization and taking over as the mastermind who pulls the strings in this school conspiracy.

In fact, she was more interested in taking down said mastermind—if one even exists.

They've been kind enough to pretend that the SOS Brigade, a mockery of a student association, doesn't exist. Haruhi should have been more appreciative and understood the position we were in, but instead, she was geared up to fight. Though at the moment, I had no idea how she intended to fight them.

However, my expectation-slash-premonition was completely off the mark, as the next challenge didn't come in the form of assassins sent by the student council.

It came from our neighbors, seeking vengeance.

THE DAY OF SAGITTARIUS

All I could see was the dark expanse of space.

It was as dark as if I'd wandered into the Horsehead Nebula with a blindfold on: there wasn't a single speck of starlight to be found. Quite frankly, this might be just a half-assed attempt at drawing a background. And here I was, hoping for some kind of flashy special effects. Well, I'm sure that even the empty void of space has its own concerns to deal with. Something along the lines of budget or technical/time constraints.

"Can't see a thing."

I muttered to no one in general. My display's been showing a black screen the entire time. I have to wonder if my monitor's broken.

As I pondered my current location in deep space, a dot of light appeared on the bottom of my empty screen and began to advance, forcing me to comment.

"Hey, Haruhi. Shouldn't you stay back a little more? Your flagship's a little too far up."

Haruhi's reply came as follows.

"Operations Officer, address me as 'Your Excellency.' As chief of

59

the SOS Brigade, I hold the same rank as a general field marshal. I'm top dog here."

I didn't even get a chance to make a wisecrack about her use of "Operations Officer" and "Your Excellency" before someone else spoke up.

"Your Excellency, Intelligence Officer Nagato has reported that the enemy armada is behaving suspiciously. Your orders?"

Koizumi delivered his status report and Haruhi gave her reply.

"It doesn't matter. We simply charge!"

A typical Haruhi order, but nobody would ever follow it. Hell, nobody did, since we all knew that a frontal assault would get us torn apart like the Takeda cavalry at Tanegashima.

Asahina had a worried look on her face as she raised her hand.

"Um…What am I supposed to do…?"

"Mikuru, you'll only get in the way, so have your supply fleet go off somewhere else, since I'm not expecting anything from you. Kyon, you join Yuki and Koizumi in taking out their vanguard. And then I'll deliver the coup de grace. With style!"

I really want somebody to stop her.

I looked back at my monitor to check on the position of my fleet, part of the SOS Brigade Space Force. The fifteen thousand vessels under my command, dubbed the <Kyon Fleet> by Haruhi, were currently advancing toward the front lines in a position directly behind the <Her Excellency☆Haruhi☆Fleet>. The <Koizumi Fleet> was flanking mine, while our consistent and steady bastion the <Yuki Fleet> was way ahead of us, scouting enemy movements. When I looked around for the <Mikuru Fleet>, which included the supply ships, I found that her shaky operation had left her lost from the beginning of the battle.

"Wah—Which way am I supposed to go?"

Asahina was practically squealing in bewilderment as she bumbled around like usual.

Any direction works. Just chill behind us, please. These ships may only exist on a screen, but I still don't want to see harm done to something with your name on it.

Suddenly the monitor before me began to display a number of changes. Data from the scouts of <Yuki Fleet> had been linked to my fleet. My screen, originally a black void with the exception of the symbols marking allied fleets, now displayed the positions of the enemy units Nagato had located.

"Stay back, Haruhi," I said. "They've split their armada. I'm guessing that they're searching for your position. The boss should behave accordingly and stay in the back lines."

"What did you say?"

Haruhi puckered her lips as she objected.

"You're going to leave me out of this? That's not fair. I want to get in there and fire beams and missiles like crazy too!"

I ordered <Kyon Fleet> to advance at a brisk pace.

"Listen up, Haruhi. If your flagship is taken out, we lose. Look. The four enemy fleets rushing us are all chumps. The flagship and its fleet are giving orders from the rear. Do you send your king rushing into the enemy when playing chess? Especially when it's the beginning of a match?"

"Well...you have a point."

Haruhi had a sullen look on her face with a tinge of bruised ego. Her eyes were locked on me as though she were a cat asking for food.

"Well then, you guys take care of it. Find the enemy flagship and bombard away. We can't lose to these punks. We're absolutely going to win. Defeat will ruin the SOS Brigade reputation. And most important of all, I wouldn't be able to stand them lording it over us!"

"Your Excellency."

Koizumi immediately made his report.

"Intelligence Officer Nagato's <Yuki Fleet> has engaged the enemy vanguard. We will soon be entering battle. I must humbly request that Your Excellency withdraw to the rear and provide the entire force with tactical leadership."

His voice sounded serious enough, but the smile on his face made it hard to believe he was sincere.

"Oh, really?"

Haruhi seemed to be very pleased by Koizumi's not-very-subtle attempt to suck up as she sat down in the brigade chief's chair with her arms crossed. The look on her face was what you would expect from a young officer straight out of the academy who'd been placed in charge because of his rank, despite his inability to provide strategic leadership.

"I'm willing to listen to the advice of Chief Officer Koizumi. Well then, work hard, everyone. Turn those impertinent computer society freaks into riddled, smoldering smithereens. Our goal is total annihilation. We're going to smash them."

I suppose that her being motivated to achieve total victory is a good thing, but she shouldn't forget that our opponents wanted this battle in space. Our enemy, the computer society, probably has the same aspirations you do.

And from what I've seen, the SOS Brigade's chances of winning were worse than the chances of the Imperial Japanese Navy at Leyte Gulf. There are no ifs in history, but assuming that you reran the scenario with equal numbers and equal forces on both sides, the IJN still would have gotten their asses handed to them. Shouldn't we just raise the white flag already?

"Well, guess we can't really do that."

I rolled up my sleeves and checked my screen again for intelligence on the enemy. Nagato's delivered again. She's provided us with data on the positions of virtually every enemy unit, with the exception of the flagship fleet. The responsibility for leading our

forces to victory rested upon my shoulders, or, namely, upon my intellect and ability as the so-called operations officer.

What to do?

"Well...then."

I stared at the flickering LCD screen on my notebook computer as I tried to come up with a plan for producing the result desired by Commander Haruhi. But first, I should probably explain our current situation. When you reach a crossroads in life, it's usually beneficial to sort out your thoughts before you confuse yourself. That's what I'll do.

It all began a week ago.

After school one autumn day.

It was a few days after the cultural festival ended, and peace and quiet had returned to the school.

That's a fairly generic introduction. Long story short, everything was back to the way it was before the festival, and I probably wasn't the only person grateful that it had ended without incident.

Though to be perfectly honest, I couldn't say for sure, since they never tell me what they're thinking, but Koizumi's smile seemed a little relieved and the absence of any expression on Nagato's face seemed to reinforce my belief.

In any case, I've begun to regard the sight of this reading machine with her head buried in a book as a symbol of peace on Earth. If I were to catch sight of Nagato behaving oddly or making a fuss, that would be a sign that I needed to write either a will or my memoirs, since it's more or less a given that nothing can happen that Nagato didn't expect. If she's sitting in the literary club room reading a foreign science fiction novel, that's solid proof I won't be waking up to a horrifying nightmare anytime soon.

Meanwhile, the beautiful girl who was from the future, despite being entirely clueless about the past, and who served as a pseudo-maid, was once again fully dressed in the attire of a domestic helper for no purpose at all and earnestly making us some steaming hot Japanese tea. I have no idea how Asahina learned the correct water temperature for the different types of tea leaves, but she'd stopped using the hot water dispenser and switched to boiling water in a kettle on the portable gas stove. She held a thermometer in one hand. Pretty sure this is the only place you're going to find a girl from the future dressed like a maid who's intently staring at a thermometer that's stuck in an open kettle. And I had a feeling she was doing it wrong, but if I started trying to name everything that was wrong, I'd probably end up finding that there wasn't anything in the SOS Brigade base that wasn't, since everything here is out of whack. The only thing normal in this room would be my awareness of my own existence. I take my hat off to Descartes.

What was once the literary club room was now an alternate space that served as headquarters for Haruhi Suzumiya and her gang. The fact that I've managed to hold on to my sanity must mean I'm someone special. On second thought, I was the only one here who didn't have a bizarre background, and the very existence of our brigade chief, Haruhi, was an enigma in itself. Something's wrong when I'm the only person with any common sense in the group.

Four crazies versus one straight man. That's not very balanced. Shouldn't there at least be one other person to share this mental strain? Besides, it's not like I enjoy playing the straight man. There are times when I'd rather not. I would gripe about the unfairness of having to shoulder this burden on my own, but I didn't particularly want to get Taniguchi or Kunikida involved in this. Not because I'd feel bad for them, but because they just aren't up to the task. I doubt they have the vocabulary or reflexes to stand against Haruhi. Come to think of it, the two of them are a bit nutty like Tsuruya. Damn it all. Crazy is the new way to go?

"Hmm."

I crossed my arms and began moaning as if deep in contemplation. It wasn't that I was having trouble figuring out what my next move should be in the game of Go I was playing with Koizumi. It wasn't very difficult to surround and take the majority of Koizumi's black stones. Don't put me on the same level as Koizumi, the board game fanatic who's horrible at everything he plays. No, I was considering if this world was actually sane, since I've reached the conclusion that you have to be insane to survive in an insane world. The normal ones will find themselves gradually losing their sanity. You have to admire how I've managed to endure the SOS Brigade clubroom, a vortex of the irrational and absurd. It's about time somebody praised me.

"Then shall I offer you words of admiration?"

At least Koizumi had the form of a master as he placed his stone on the board and removed one of my white stones. He could play with the best of them, but he didn't notice that it would only be a matter of time before his move came back to haunt him.

"I'll pass."

That was my response as I dipped my fingers into my bowl of stones and shuffled them around, gauging what seemed to be a sincere expression of admiration on Koizumi's face. It failed to bring me any joy, so I continued in a lethargic voice.

"It wouldn't feel good coming from you. I'll just end up worried that there's a catch somewhere. Just to be clear, I'm not a pawn in your game. If you expect me to act the way you people want, then you've got another think coming."

"I can't help but wonder which one of our factions your statement is referring to, but you have it all wrong. You and Suzumiya have been completely unpredictable every step of the way. My presence here would be proof of that."

If Koizumi had never transferred to this school, Haruhi would never have recruited him to be a member of the SOS Brigade. She was never interested in Itsuki Koizumi's gender, personality, character, or appearance. All she cared about was the fact that he was a transfer student. He was pretty much screwed after transferring to this school at an unusual time of year. Or maybe he transferred here on purpose to get closer to Haruhi. Yet considering how he happens to be one of those espers Haruhi is looking for, his situation would be akin to that of a person living next to radioactive material and having to constantly worry about a Chernobyl that can't be predicted. It's possible that he actually wanted to stay as far away from her as he could.

"In the past, perhaps."

Koizumi stared at the Go stone in his hand.

"The original plan was to observe her from a distance. Thus, I was terrified when Suzumiya first came to see me and brought me to this clubroom after school. And then she announced that our goal was to find aliens, time travelers, and espers and have fun with them. I could only laugh."

Koizumi sounded a bit nostalgic as he reminisced.

"But it's different now. I may have started off as an enigmatic transfer student, but that description no longer applies to me. I'm sure that Suzumiya agrees."

So what? You're still an enigma as far as I'm concerned.

Koizumi looked around the clubroom, stopping at Nagato, reading in the corner of the room like a cat that prefers narrow places, before moving on to Asahina, still staring intently at the kettle, and finally returning to me.

Haruhi wasn't around. She was on classroom cleaning duty. Otherwise, Koizumi and I wouldn't be relaxing here and having a leisurely conversation.

So we were sitting around the clubroom without the brigade chief present, and Koizumi was smiling the way an experienced veterinarian would smile at an injured small bird.

"Nagato, Asahina, me, and you, of course. We are all sanctioned members of the SOS Brigade. Nothing more, nothing less. I'm sure that's how Suzumiya feels about it."

Is there a point in judging if someone is more or less than a member of the SOS Brigade?

"Absolutely. Extraordinary entities such as aliens and sliders would be worth more. Ordinary humans who aren't brigade members would be worth less."

So Taniguchi, Kunikida, Tsuruya, and my sister would all be worth less than brigade members? Not that I'm trying to defend them, but it would pain me to think that they're worth less than I am.

"The logic is simple. If Suzumiya considered them important, they would be here with us right now as fellow members. Their absence shows that Suzumiya doesn't consider them important. She values them as much as a random ordinary person walking by. As they say, hindsight is twenty-twenty."

"What about sliders? None have showed up yet?"

"In hindsight, I would say that none currently exist in this world. For if any existed, he or she would inevitably have been summoned to this room by chance."

"That's a good thing. I'm not interested in running off to an alternate dimension."

As I placed a white stone on the board to eliminate a considerable number of Koizumi's pieces, all but assuring victory, a teacup was placed next to the Go board.

"I'm sorry about the wait. Here's your tea."

Asahina was standing next to us with a smile you'd expect to find on a coach who had led a scrappy Little League baseball team to a regional championship.

"I bought these Karigane leaves for the first time. I think I was able to brew it well...It was expensive, though."

It is a travesty that you have to pay out of your own pocket. You should ask Haruhi to reimburse you later. Well, it really isn't necessary to splurge on tea leaves. Even tap water, once graced by Asahina's hands, would taste better than Evian mineral water.

"Hee hee, drink it slowly."

It was clear that Asahina had become accustomed to wearing her maid costume as she placed a teacup in front of Koizumi before turning to gracefully carry the tray with the remaining teacup over to Nagato.

"..."

Nagato showed no reaction, just as always, but it appeared that no reaction was less of a strain on Asahina than an actual expression of gratitude. I have yet to see the SOS Brigade alien and time traveler engage in a friendly conversation. Actually, I've never seen Nagato have a pleasant conversation with anybody. Well, I guess that's fine. It'd be scary if Nagato suddenly started jabbering away, and a waste if she turned into another Haruhi, who just needs to shut up.

If someone never talks and doesn't make any trouble, we should keep it that way.

After spending some time playing Go and sipping my tea, I could almost forget about the evil in this world. However, this pedestrian moment of peace didn't last long, as trouble, afraid of being forgotten, has a habit of rearing its ugly head on a regular basis.

There was a knock on the door. I looked up at the scratched, cheap door and steeled myself. For what? The four brigade members who weren't Haruhi were currently lounging around the clubroom. And Haruhi would be the last person in the world to show manners and knock on the door. Which meant that the person on the other side wasn't Haruhi or another member of the SOS Brigade, but an outsider. No idea who it was, but I could use my masterful powers of deduction to conclude that he or she was bringing us some kind of mess to deal with. See Kimidori a few months ago.

"Yes, coming right away!"

I could hear Asahina shuffling toward the door. She's become so used to this routine that she no longer questions why she's acting like a maid. Is that...a good thing?

"Ah?!"

Asahina apparently saw someone unexpected after opening the door. Her eyes were wide open.

"Welcome...P-please come in?"

Asahina took two steps back as she covered her chest with her arms for some reason.

"No, I'll stay out here."

Our visitor sounded a little nervous as he stuck his head through the doorway and looked around the room.

"The brigade chief isn't around, huh..."

The speaker, who was unable to conceal the relief in his voice, was the leader of our neighbors, the computer society president.

No one else made a move, so I had to serve as the receptionist. Asahina was frozen in place, Koizumi was simply smiling at the upperclassman, and Nagato had yet to look away from her book.

"How may we help you?"

He's an upperclassman. I should probably show some respect. I stood up and stepped in front of Asahina in a semblance of shielding her. Hmm? The computer society president, standing right outside the doorway, was followed by a cluster of male students who seemed to hover, like a bunch of ancestral spirits that were haunting him. What's up? It's the wrong time of year for a vendetta attack.

The president appeared to relax upon seeing that I was the one

who stepped forward, as a thin smile spread across his face and he straightened his back.

"First, I'd like you to take this."

I didn't really understand why he was holding out a CD case to me. Why would I accept it? The computer society had no reason to give us any presents without an ulterior motive, so naturally I was skeptical.

"No, this isn't anything dangerous," said the president. "You'll find game software inside. It's an original we developed. We released it at the cultural festival just the other day. Did you happen to see it?"

Sorry, but I didn't have time. The only memories I want to retain from the cultural festival are those of the band performance and Asahina's waitress costume.

"I see…"

The president wasn't offended, but his shoulders slumped as he mumbled something about their display's being in a bad spot. If you just came here to chat, you should finish up and get going. Don't blame me if Haruhi shows up and turns this into a big fight.

"But of course, I came here for a reason. But I agree that I should probably make it quick. Here I go then!"

The president appeared to be perspiring profusely as the band of spectators behind him nodded solemnly. I really wish he would hurry it up.

"We challenge you to a contest at this game!"

The president's voice cracked as he thrust the CD case at me again.

Why would we want to play a game against the computer society? If you don't have anybody to play with, I would advise that you try a different clubroom.

"This is no simple game."

The president appeared to be dug in for a fight.

"This is a contest. We even have a wager prepared."

I'll give you Koizumi, then. You can have your little contest in the computer society clubroom.

"You're missing the point. We want to have a contest with you guys!"

I'm begging you. Stop yelling "contest" over and over. Who knows if your shouting has reached Haruhi's sharp ears? If that girl, baseless self-confidence incarnate, happens to catch that word—

"Booya!"

"Guh-oh!"

That bizarre sequence happened as somebody came in from the side and sent the president flying out of sight.

"Whoa?!" "Prez!" "Are you okay?!"

Followed a few seconds later by his fellow members' crying out and racing over to where the president was sprawled in the hallway. I slowly turned my gaze to the side.

"Who are you people?"

A girl stood there with her finely shaped lips in a wide smile and shining eyes directed toward the computer society members. Haruhi Suzumiya herself.

After her sneak flying kick on the president, Haruhi had executed a ten-point landing and now stood there with a triumphant look on her face.

Haruhi brushed away a lock of hair from her ear.

"So the evil organization has finally come. You must belong to some secret organization that finds the SOS Brigade a nuisance. I won't let you have your way. It is our duty as the good guys to bring light where there is darkness and vanquish all that is evil. You peons should let me one-up you already!"

The president had apparently hit his head when he took a tumble, as he lay there moaning with his subordinates fussing over him. I was probably the only one who heard Haruhi's little speech.

"Hey, Haruhi."

I don't even want to try to count how many times I've had to calm her down since starting high school.

"Why don't you listen before kicking people around? Just look. Now nobody knows what's going on. All I heard was that he wanted to challenge us to a contest at some game."

"Kyon, a contest begins the second someone challenges you. A declaration of hostile intent is the same as a declaration of war. Anything the loser says otherwise is merely an excuse. Nobody wants to hear a loser whine."

Haruhi walked over to the president like a hunter inspecting her freshly bagged prey before expressing obvious disappointment in a somewhat churlish gesture.

"Oh. It's just our neighbors. Why did these guys come here picking a fight?"

Like I said, they were just about to explain that. You ambushed him from the side before he had a chance to talk.

"But," Haruhi pouted, "I thought that the student council had come to demand that we surrender this clubroom. I'm expecting them to show up anytime now. Honestly, don't make things so difficult."

"That doesn't make it okay for you to kick people."

I attempted to scold Haruhi.

"Come to think of it, we haven't tried that event yet…"

This came from Koizumi, who at some point had moved from his position in the doorway to join us in the hallway. He appeared to be deep in thought, so I stepped on his toes. Don't say anything that'll make this worse.

"Ugh…craven SOS Brigade…"

The president continued to moan as he finally managed to stand up with his fellow members supporting him.

"I-in any case, the contest is on. I was expecting there to be some

communication difficulties, so I wrote everything down. You should understand the contest after reading these documents."

One of the computer society members walked over carrying a stack of copy paper and CD cases and looking like he was in the process of feeding fresh meat to wild lions.

"Appreciate it."

Koizumi accepted the items with a smile on his face.

"I understand that we'll be playing a game, but is there an instruction manual that comes with it?"

A different member walked over to hand Koizumi another stack of paper, before speaking quietly.

"Prez, we're done here. Let's return to the clubroom."

"Yes, let's."

A weak nod.

"Well, there you have it—"

The president attempted to depart after giving his half-assed explanation, but Haruhi grabbed him by the neck.

"Give us a proper explanation. I won't let you trick me with a bunch of fine print. Give a thorough explanation that even stupid Kyon here could understand!"

Who are you calling stupid?

The unfortunate president was dragged into the literary club room. The remaining computer society members had no time to voice any objections or rescue their president before the door was shut on them.

The cultural festival period of celebration was over and unlike Haruhi, who had fireworks going off in her head year-round, the rest of the school had returned to everyday life, or so I thought. However, it appeared that the computer society was still in a festive mood. Still, as I looked at the president, cowering in a metal chair all by his lonesome, he reminded me of a white mage with no magic points left and surrounded by zombies after getting separated from the rest of his party on the last floor of a dungeon. He hadn't even touched the tea prepared by the similarly cowering Asahina as he sat through Haruhi's interrogation.

I'll give a brief summary.

The president's demands were as follows.

1. Accept our challenge to a contest using a game made by the computer society.
2. If we win, return the computer that is currently sitting on the SOS Brigade desk to its original place.
3. Besides, the SOS Brigade doesn't need an advanced multi-function computer. Computers are meant to be used by the computer society and we insist on its return.
4. In this case, I'm willing to forget the mental anguish I suffered during the computer extortion. No, I want to forget. Let's all forget it ever happened.
5. And the reasons stated above obligate you to accept our challenge. Fight us.

The sheets of paper Koizumi passed around basically explained the above in writing that was hard to understand and printed in a font that wasn't very legible. An accusation and challenge bundled into one, I guess. I skimmed the neatly typewritten discourse, but Haruhi made the president talk. Long story short,

"If you aren't using the computer, give it back."

Per the president. Haruhi sounded shocked as she responded.

"I'm using it. All the time. The editing for the movie was done on this."

Except I'm the one who did it.

"And the home page too."

That was also me. Haruhi has only ever used the computer to

surf the Web when she was bored and to design that scribble of an emblem.

"It's been six months and your home page is nothing more than an index page. It hasn't been updated in months."

The president was quite upset. Well, I guess he was the one who kept the access counter moving regularly on that pathetic site. I see. That explains the cave cricket incident. He really wanted to know if we were making use of the computer.

"But when I told you to give me the computer, you agreed. Kyon, you remember, right?"

Was that how it went? I could remember Asahina lying prostrate on the floor, but I didn't pay much attention to what the president said. Even if we assume that he agreed, any deal you reached would probably be invalid, given his state of mental retardation at the time.

"I strongly object."

The president appeared to be serious about this. He had his arms crossed and his lips were pursed in what was apparently his best attempt to look tough. You'd figure that he'd have given up after six months, but it seems that his rage had made a resurgence.

Haruhi just snorted and gave him a little nod with a smile on her face.

"Very well. If you want a contest so badly, I'll go along with it. We're putting our computer on the line. So what will your side be wagering?"

"What? We're wagering this computer. If we lose, we'll let you keep the computer."

Haruhi's response was cool.

"This already belongs to us. Why would I want to receive something that already belongs to us? Bring something else."

I couldn't help but be impressed by her gusto. Once an object came to be in her possession, no matter the circumstances or the legitimacy of her claim, it belonged to her permanently. Does she plan on growing up to be a thief?

However, the president merely smiled, albeit stiffly, instead of getting angry.

"I understand. A new offer...that's right. How about new computers for each member? I'll give you four of them. Are you fine with laptops?"

He voluntarily offered to raise the stakes. This appeared to surprise Haruhi.

"Huh, really?"

She hopped off her seat on the brigade chief desk and peered at the president's face.

"For real? I won't let you go back on your word later."

"I won't. Promise. I'm willing to sign in blood."

The president was still acting tough. Made sense to me.

I wasn't sure about the content of the game that was on the CD Nagato was staring at, but the producers must know the game inside out. Setting aside the issue of whether or not the computer society members are all skilled gamers, they're probably expecting to have an easy time kicking around the amateurs of the SOS Brigade. I'd have to agree. I doubt we'd have a chance in any fair contest. We only won the baseball game because of Nagato's unreal powers. It had nothing to do with our own capabilities.

But somebody didn't know that.

"You don't have any female members, do you?"

Haruhi asked a rather odd question.

"No, what of it?" asked the president.

"Do you want any female members?"

"...No, not really."

The president was trying hard to maintain his bluff while Haruhi leered at him like the mistress of an establishment of ill repute.

"If you win, I'll give this girl to the computer society."

She pointed at Nagato's face.

"You want a girl around, right? Yuki will definitely be useful right off the bat. She's got a good memory and she's the best-behaved person in the room."

You idiot. That's a horrible suggestion. You're thinking that it wouldn't be fair to bet our one computer against four of theirs? But there's a huge difference in the specs between four computers and Nagato. Not that you would know.

"..."

Nagato didn't even flinch as Haruhi offered her up as a prize. Her static eyes gave me a short glance before passing over Haruhi to stare at the computer society president's face.

The president was clearly disturbed, judging by the look on his face.

"Uh…but…"

"What? You would rather have Mikuru? Or you think that four computers wouldn't be enough? Then if we win, you also have to change the name of your club to North High SOS Brigade Two."

"Ah…um…well…"

Haruhi's words had left Asahina paralyzed in place with her hand covering her mouth.

"You be the prize."

I walked over to Haruhi in a fit of rage.

"Stop treating Nagato and Asahina like they're objects. Why don't you bet your own body? Don't just say what you want."

"What are you talking about? The SOS Brigade chief is a holy and sacred symbol. You could even say that I am the brigade. I have no intention of yielding this position to anyone who doesn't make an instant impression on me."

You plan on loitering around here after you've graduated?

"Besides, you won't be able to find anything in this world that can equal me in value."

Haruhi sidestepped my criticism with her unreasonable statements, pointed to the reticent Nagato and speechless Asahina, and returned to putting pressure on the president.

"So, which one do you want?"

She then gave me a sidelong glance before continuing.

"If you insist, well, you can take me."

As expected, the president didn't take Haruhi up on her nonsense. Based on my careful observation, he seemed to linger on Nagato for a while. I can understand that.

He was guilty of previously groping Asahina's breasts, and I doubt he had the guts to pick the victim of his crime. Besides, Nagato had plenty of secret admirers, according to Taniguchi, so it was possible that he happened to have a thing for the quiet bookish type. Though it was also possible that he wouldn't be able to relax with Asahina around. At least he was able to keep himself from begging for female members, so this was more or less the obvious outcome.

Oh, Haruhi? Now that everyone knows what her personality is like, you'd have to be a bona fide masochist or complete weirdo to pick her. And you're not going to find anybody weirder than Haruhi. Which is why I don't worry about guys taking advantage of her.

And so the stage was set for our battle.

The president left the literary club room briefly before returning with his posse. They were carrying what could only be notebook computers. I was about to say that it was rather generous of them to give us our prizes beforehand, but this game apparently required each team to have five computers. They were so fast in hooking up Haruhi's desktop and the four laptops to the LAN and installing the homemade game software that I had to wonder if they were computer society members or telecom techs. By listening to their conversation, I was able to learn that the match would be a 5v5 online space battle simulation. Basically, the SOS Brigade needed five computers, the computer society needed five computers, and all of them would be hooked up to the same server for the contest. We would be in our clubroom and they would be in theirs.

Naturally, the server computer would be in their clubroom. Uh-huh, I get it.

"One week of practice time should be enough."

The president looked pleased as he watched the computer society members work swiftly.

"The battle will commence one week from today at 4 PM. Polish up your skills in the meantime. It'll be disappointing if you're too weak."

He thinks that he's already won, though the same could be said of Haruhi. She can't stop herself from gloating about the new computers.

"Uh-huh, I was thinking about looking into acquiring some mini-notebooks. Every brigade member should have a computer. Investment in equipment is critical for boosting the motivation to work."

My motivation isn't going to sell itself for a laptop. Though I'll be happy to take it.

I drank my now-cold tea and casually looked over at the expression on Nagato's face. Or lack of expression, I should say. No visible change as she stood with Asahina against the wall and watched the computer society members, as calm as usual.

This game was produced by their side. I seriously doubt that they would plant a suspect virus, but you never know. Nagato would say something if that were the case. I can let her handle that stuff. The computer society won't be able to easily pull a fast one on Nagato.

As I fidgeted with my empty teacup, Asahina walked over.

"Kyon, um...what are they doing exactly? I'm, well, not very familiar with m-machines..."

She stared at the increasing number of wires with a distressed look on her face. You really don't need to worry so much about it.

"It's only a game. Just play around with it."

I attempted to comfort her. Though to be honest, that was how I actually felt about the whole thing. If Nagato and Asahina had actually been on the line in this contest, then I wouldn't hesitate to unleash the power within. But if we're fighting over whether or not Haruhi has to return the computer she stole, it's a different story. The computer society's demands were low-risk, high-return as far as I was concerned. Just goes to show that they're confident enough to give us a considerable handicap.

"This is one contest where we have nothing to lose and everything to gain. I won't let Haruhi bitch us around this time."

I flashed a smile at Asahina as I made a firm assertion to assuage her fears.

"But Suzumiya...She seems so enthusiastic about this."

Haruhi didn't even wait for the computer society members to leave before sitting down at her brigade chief desk and grabbing hold of the mouse with Koizumi standing at her side, holding what was apparently the instruction manual.

The president and the rest of our neighbors looked very pleased with themselves for some reason as they left. They must have done a fine piece of work.

Afterward we spent a while trying out our computers, but the sun was getting low in the sky so we called it a day.

As the five of us left school together, Koizumi and I had a conversation. We were a few yards behind the three girls as we descended the hill, and I was the one who spoke first.

"There's a phrase that I've been meaning to retire."

"Oh? What might that be?"

"Take a guess."

Koizumi smiled mockingly before contemplating for a moment.

"If I were in your position, there wouldn't be many phrases that could see abuse. The silent '...' and the 'give me a break' variant would be strong contenders. Wouldn't these be the only possibilities?"

I kept my mouth shut as Koizumi flashed that everlasting smile of his and stated the correct answer.

"Good grief."

I'm guessing that the shrug and spreading of his arms were something extra he threw in. Koizumi gestured with his arms as he continued speaking.

"I understand how you feel."

The hell you do.

"You misunderstand. I mean that you are attempting to avoid falling into a state of routine, correct? If you are forced to react in the same way on a regular basis, the process would grow tedious for you, if not other people. It is similar to how you cannot bring yourself to touch a game that you've already replayed many times over again. You fear tedium. Suzumiya feels the same way. The difference would be that she actively comes up with activities to engage in while you simply react to her actions. Now, which side would have an easier time?"

Why are you talking like a shrink? Don't try to explain my mental state with your funny theories. Besides, if you want to talk motive, you should look in the mirror. Koizumi is more or less passive when Haruhi's involved.

"We are here of our own volition. Have you forgotten? Nagato, Asahina, and I may follow different doctrines, but we are all here for the same purpose. I shouldn't need to tell you that we have the vital task of observing Suzumiya."

Meaning that I was the only person who'd been dragged into the SOS Brigade without a purpose and forced to run around in circles. Seriously, who's behind this mess?

"I wouldn't know."

Koizumi gave me an amused look.

"Speaking of which, Suzumiya is no longer our only target of observation. You have been included. While I remain fearful of the havoc you and Suzumiya may wreak, I have been given an opportunity to open my mind, which I truly appreciate. No, I do not jest. I am very grateful."

Must be fun to watch other people suffer.

The seasons must have straightened themselves out during the cultural festival, as the mountain winds carried an autumn chill. A season I couldn't stand. When I realized that it would only get colder from here on out, I was tempted to think that I'd rather suffer Haruhi's oppression.

The sky had grown dark as Haruhi jabbered away by herself ahead of us in a cluster with Asahina, who occasionally nodded in agreement, and Nagato, whose functional capacity was apparently limited to walking when heading home from school. Nagato's bag was bulging because it contained the laptop she had received. When I asked her why she was taking it home with her, she merely slipped the game CD into the bottom of her bag and said that she was going to "analyze" it. As I watched her silhouette, a thought crossed my mind.

"By the way, Koizumi. I have a suggestion to make."

"How unusual. I can't wait to hear it."

I lowered my voice to be safe.

"About the contest with the computer society. Can we skip the cheating this time?"

"What do you mean by cheating?"

Koizumi also responded in a soft voice.

"Anything like what Nagato did during the baseball game."

Don't tell me you forgot.

"I want to make this clear up front. If you happen to have a special power that gives you an advantage at simulation games, don't use it. This isn't limited to special powers. I won't allow the use of any gimmicks that are against the rules."

Koizumi smiled as he shot me a questioning look.

"What are you expecting to happen? Do you mean to say that it's all right for us to lose?"

"That's right."

I conceded that point.

"For once, all cosmic stuff, future stuff, or ESP is off-limits. Fight honestly and accept the honest result. That would be the best way."

"I would like to know your reasoning."

"The only thing we'll lose is the computer we stole. And it'll be returned to its original owner. That won't hurt us."

Though I'll need to move the Asahina image collection somewhere first.

"I'm not concerned about the computer."

Koizumi sounded amused.

"You should know that Suzumiya doesn't like to lose. If she feels that all is lost and defeat is near, she will produce closed space and cause another rampage that nobody is aware of. You don't mind if this happens?"

"I don't care."

I glanced at Haruhi's back.

"She has to learn her lesson one of these days. She can't have her way all the time. Especially since Haruhi isn't the instigator this time. She shouldn't be too concerned about the outcome."

I'll need to tell Nagato tomorrow that supernatural powers will be off-limits. Guess I should also tell Asahina. I seriously doubt that she has access to any exceptional powers or items, since she confessed to being completely clueless about machines, but just to be safe.

Koizumi chuckled softly. The hell was that? You're creeping me out.

"No, I wasn't laughing at you. I was just feeling envious."

Envious of what?

"Of the invisible bond of trust between you and Suzumiya."

I have no idea what you're talking about.

"You're going to feign ignorance? No, it's possible that you don't realize how Suzumiya trusts you and you, in turn, trust her."

How would you know who I trust?

"Let us assume that we lose the game next week. However, you believe that Suzumiya will not produce closed space as a result. This would be an example of your trust. Likewise, Suzumiya also believes that you will surely lead us to victory. Another example of trust. She was willing to bet brigade members because she genuinely believes that we cannot lose. Neither of you may express it in words, but the two of you are connected by an almost ideal bond of trust."

I fell into a well of silence. Why didn't I have a response for him? Because Koizumi's speculation more or less hit the nail on the head? I'll let the experts handle the question of whether or not I trust her, but it's true that I don't expect a rampage to break out in Haruhi's mental world. This is a good thing when you consider what's happened over the past six months. Many things have happened during the period between the founding of the SOS Brigade and the movie filming. Personally, I would say that I've matured a bit over the past few months, so I'm sure that the same could be said for Haruhi, who essentially had the same experiences I did. Or else she'd be a true idiot in every sense of the word. Beyond help.

"It's worth a shot."

I finally managed to string together a response.

"If we lose this game to the computer society and Haruhi ends up creating that disturbing gray world again, you can count me out of your scheme. I'm going to join Haruhi in messing up the world."

Koizumi merely smiled. And then he continued in a matter-of-fact tone.

"This shows the trust you share. Do you now understand the source of my envy?"

I didn't respond as I focused on trudging along the path. Koizumi looked like he had something else to add, but he must have sensed that I wasn't interested in listening, since he kept his mouth shut.

Oh well. I'm used to Koizumi's insinuating looks. They were as commonplace as Asahina's wearing a maid outfit in the clubroom or Haruhi's bursting with baseless confidence.

Or Nagato's being so low-profile that you could never tell if she was around... which was another parallel that came to mind—

But I would witness something completely unexpected during the match with the computer society a week later.

And so our training began the next day against virtual opponents representing our neighbors. Though our training basically consisted of playing games, I should probably give a brief introduction to the original game made by the computer society.

<The Day of Sagittarius 3>.

That was the title of the game. It feels like they were going for something that sounded cool, but ended up with something that doesn't make sense. Still, the actual game is what matters here, since the SOS Brigade name isn't better by any means. I doubt there are many groups on this planet that can beat us when it comes to having a meaningless name and a pointless purpose. Still, the 3 would suggest that there were also a 1 and a 2.

In any case, I'll start by explaining the background setting of <The Day of Sagittarius 3>—

I don't know what year it was. Though it was probably sometime in the distant future. The human race had ventured into outer space to expand its territory considerably. This was an interplanetary territorial conflict that was occurring in a certain star system. There were two galactic powers in this sector engaged in a border dispute with no end in sight. For convenience's sake, we'll call one side the <Computer Society Federation> and the other side the <SOS Empire>. Each nation was armed with its own fleet of spaceships, as warfare was conducted in the void of space, and a critical situation was intensifying as both sides sent all available forces to the front lines because this inane battle would continue until the credits rolled. There were no diplomatic or strategic commands to interfere with raw combat. Total annihilation was the only solution. This game sounds like it's right up Haruhi's alley.

The screen was completely dark at the start of the game. The blue flashing dots at the bottom of the monitor represented the fleet units we controlled. I could see a total of five isosceles triangles that had a shorter bottom edge lined up together. This was the entire force of the <SOS Empire>, led by Haruhi. Each unit represented fifteen thousand spaceships, for a total of seventy-five thousand, plus a few extra supply vessels. We would satisfy the conditions for victory by controlling our ships to destroy an enemy armada of a similar size, or in the case of the special rules for this match, the enemy commander's fleet. In other words, we would lose, regardless of the damage or losses suffered by the rest of the armada, if the flagship of <Her Excellency☆Haruhi☆Fleet> was taken out, and our opponents would lose if the flagship of the president's fleet was destroyed.

Each person was assigned a fleet in the armada, which meant that my fleet could only be controlled from my own computer.

I wouldn't be able to do anything from my laptop if and when Haruhi ran off by herself.

One of the odd features of this game was the fact that you had to do a thorough search to learn not only the position of the enemy, but any potential obstacles in the terrain. In any case, if we wanted to move into a different sector, we would have to dispatch scouts on a scan and wait for them to return before we could learn anything about our surroundings. Pretty convoluted.

Each fleet had its own field of vision, which was only an area with a radius of a few centimeters (on the screen), so if you were to advance without scouting ahead, you might find yourself under attack from an unexpected direction with no way of knowing where the enemy was.

However, all data was linked between allied fleets (at least, that's how it was supposed to work), so, for example, the field of vision for Nagato's fleet along with any data retrieved by her scout vessels would be shared with the rest of us. The game was set up so I could sit around and stare at the faint illumination of my field of vision on the black screen while learning the locations of planets and asteroid belts as well as enemy positions.

Still, the map was so big that the battle would be determined by one side's swiftly determining the enemy's position and taking action.

There were two types of weapons available, beams and missiles. Beams would hit enemies as soon as they were in range, while missiles were slower but came with a homing function. Missiles were impossible to evade, so you had to shoot each one down.

Generally speaking, this was a 2D fleet simulation game set in space. And this was in real time, not turn-based, so if you wasted too much time searching around the stars, you'd eventually find yourself surrounded by enemies. That aspect of the game was rather unforgiving.

*   *   *

In preparation for the upcoming contest, we got started on our week of gaming. Haruhi was the only one with a desktop computer at her desk while the rest of us sat along the table and stared at our laptops while mouse-clicking furiously. This surreal scene would be a part of SOS Brigade activity for a while. We were practicing against the computer instead of actual opponents, but it still took us three days before we could even score a win with the difficulty set to very easy. Our gaming skills were creeping along as fast as it would take to dig below Earth's mantle with a hand drill.

"Ah! I got blown up again! Kyon, this game is starting to piss me off."

Pretty pathetic showing against a computer opponent. Haruhi wasn't the only one getting ticked off, but the problem here wasn't game balance. The problem is that you keep charging forward with your flagship to get bombarded by concentrated enemy fire.

"Though we also need to change our strategy."

I looked away from the LCD monitor, which showed a GAME OVER screen accompanied by mournful music.

"We should probably readjust the parameters for each fleet. Especially for your flagship fleet."

Each fleet unit can assign three combat parameters. [Speed], [Defense], and [Attack]. Each player starts with 100 points, which are allocated among the three parameters on the start screen. Something like [Speed · 30], [Defense · 40], [Attack · 30]. And Haruhi was playing with her parameters set to [Speed · 50], [Defense · 0], [Attack · 50], so the armor on her flagship was thin as cardboard. I was dying to tell her to show more respect for outer space. In any case, it was clear that she only cared about smashing enemy ships as quickly as possible. We aren't going to make any progress if Haruhi gets her flagship totaled before Koizumi and I have a chance to do anything.

"Man! This is such a pain. What's the point in making a game that's no fun? I like things that are easy to understand!"

Despite her grumbling, Haruhi continued to start up another game. I didn't comment as the <The Day of Sagittarius 3> logo appeared on the screen of my laptop.

Haruhi cheerfully clicked away with her mouse as she talked.

"They should have made an RPG instead. They would represent the Devil or some evil god while I play the hero. I would prefer a game where the last boss fight starts right after the opening scene. I've always wondered why the boss waits at the end of a dungeon instead of showing up at the very beginning. That's what I would do if I were the Devil. The hero wouldn't have to waste a bunch of time wandering around a dungeon this way, and the story would end quickly."

I ignored Haruhi's nonsense as I looked around at the other members. Chief Officer Koizumi sat closest to Haruhi, then me, Asahina next to me, and Nagato at the end of the table.

"This is rather difficult. Well, it may simply be my lack of familiarity with such games. The design itself is simple, but the controls are insane."

The pointless commentary by Koizumi was accompanied by the same easy smile he always had when we played Othello. Meanwhile, Asahina was wearing her maid outfit when there wasn't any need.

"Wah-wah, my flashing light won't move the way I'm telling it to. Why are we limited to moving in two dimensions when this takes place in space?"

She asked a very fundamental question as she fumbled around with her mouse.

These two wouldn't be a problem. The remaining member was my primary concern at the moment.

"…"

Yuki Nagato stared at her monitor the way a mathematician

would stare at an extremely advanced math problem. She was the first to adapt to this game: our only victory, which came despite Haruhi's method of recklessly charging forward in a straight line, could be attributed to her precise execution of fleet maneuvers.

Naturally, I'd warned her beforehand that she shouldn't use any magic or data manipulation or super-underhanded tricks. I took care of that piece of business during lunch. Nagato's response had been to look me in the eye for a few seconds before nodding wordlessly in assent, which helped to lighten the burden on my shoulders. Consequently, I didn't need to worry about the game ahead of us. If we actually managed to win, it would be the result of some kind of mistake, and that wouldn't be for me to deal with. Yep, I already have an excuse prepared for shirking any responsibility.

All that's left is to come up with a strategy that lets us put up a good fight so we can be defeated in a blaze of glory. And I can't forget about burning the Asahina image folder onto a CD.

The week flew by in a hectic mess that befit these closing days of autumn, and it was finally time for the battle to begin.

Our little group, led by Haruhi, sat down at our respective seats in the literary club room while the computer society members sat in their clubroom and everybody watched the countdown on the screens.

As we waited for the game to begin, our monitors displayed a brief introduction of each armada. The only visible information consisted of names and which fleet the flagship was in. Parameters and distribution were hidden.

Beginning with the flagship fleet, the computer society's units had been assigned the personal names <Dies Irae>, <Equinox>, <Lupercalia>, <Blindness>, and <Muspelheim>.

Their naming sense was brazen enough to give me the impression that their baffling efforts were misdirected, to say the least. It soon became clear that I wasn't the only one who had no interest in the origin of those names.

"It's too much effort to remember their names, so we'll call them A, B, C, D, and E from left to right. The flagship fleet is A."

Haruhi instantly changed the code names for the enemy armada, as she clearly had no plans to remember those vainglorious names. I wished she would forget about the <Kyon Fleet> under my command while she was at it.

"It's almost time. Listen up, everyone. We're in it to win. This is only the beginning. The computer society is not our only enemy. We must eliminate all obstacles so the SOS Brigade will be known in the far reaches of the universe. Eventually, I'll negotiate with the Department of Education to create chapters of the SOS Brigade in every public high school. One must have ambition."

I have no idea how everybody interpreted Haruhi's megalomaniacal manifesto, but Koizumi merely brushed his thumb across his lips while Asahina tugged at the sleeve of her maid outfit and Nagato's eyebrows may have twitched.

"Well, it's impossible for us to lose. But even if we've all but won already, nobody is allowed to hold back! A halfhearted victory would only be an insult to our opponent. We must crush them."

I've always wondered what this confidence of hers is made of. Two milligrams will do, so share some with me.

"Really? Want me to inject a bit into you?"

I had no idea what was going on as Haruhi suddenly glared at me. Don't stare at me with such a serious look on your face. It's not like a winning lottery ticket is going to pop out of my mouth.

After ten seconds or so of this bizarre ritual, I was forced to avert my eyes.

"Well? Didn't that help?"

Haruhi had a pleased smile on her face. What effect was staring at me supposed to have?

"I focused energy into my stare to send to you. Don't you feel your body getting all warm or going through accelerated perspiration? Yeah, this is what I'll do the next time I spot someone who's looking down."

Please don't glare at random people on a crowded street. In my mind I ran a simulation of having to run away from a gang of thugs after Haruhi's attempt to inject energy was mistaken for a challenge.

"It's almost time to start."

Koizumi's amused voice drew my eyes back to the computer screen. Asahina was the only person showing any signs of nervous strain as she murmured to herself in an anxious voice.

"...What to do? I don't think I can do this."

You don't need to get so serious about a game where there aren't any casualties. And if there *are* any casualties, they'll be limited to a few monitors that were the victims of a nasty temper.

We can only pray that Haruhi won't be so mad about losing that she throws the computer out the window.

1600 hours.

The fanfare that signaled the commencement of hostilities played and so began the battle over ownership of a computer.

Here was the initial strategy of the <SOS Empire> forces.

The <Yuki Fleet> was in the vanguard, flanked by the <Koizumi Fleet> and the <Kyon Fleet>, with the <Mikuru Fleet> and the <Her Excellency☆Haruhi☆Fleet> bringing up the rear.

—That was it. Nothing more, nothing less.

Haruhi couldn't be bothered to dispatch scout vessels, as she was only focused on destroying the enemy armada. It was clear that she wouldn't be any help until we encountered enemies.

And then we had Asahina, who wasn't going to be any help

period. We'd dumped everybody else's supply vessels on her, which meant that the triangle representing the <Mikuru Fleet> unit was somewhat larger than everybody else's. This also meant that her fleet was slower than everyone else's, so I gave her the order to take the most logical course of action and run away the second she was about to get caught up in a skirmish. Pretty obvious.

I should mention that Haruhi's fleet had been set to the parameters [Speed · 20], [Defense · 60], [Attack · 20]. Basically, we would lose the instant her units were destroyed, so we had no choice but to prioritize defense. The plan was for the combatants—Nagato, Koizumi, and me, who were running 33, 33, 34, a balanced distribution—to fight on the front lines while Haruhi chilled in the back to buy us time. But the second I took my eyes off her, we ended up in the situation at the start of this story, where she kept trying to charge ahead.

And now, as I mentioned briefly in the beginning, the simulation game between the computer society and the SOS Brigade was about to see its first combat.

"Fine, then. I'll stay back for now, so you better beat the crap out of our opponents. Mikuru, you can watch the show with me."

"Oh…you're right."

Asahina nodded meekly from her position on my left before whispering softly to me in a sweet and breathy voice.

"Please do your best, Kyon."

Her words of encouragement were enough to spur me into a hundred different ways of exerting myself. If the flagship fleet in our armada had been the <Mikuru Fleet>, I would have been more than happy to eat every missile that came her way. Unfortunately, I was obligated to serve a tyrannical despot who would have been the first warlord to start a revolt during the feudal period. It's too bad that this game doesn't come with the option to switch sides. I don't have a choice. I can only focus on dealing with the enemies before me.

*　　　*　　　*

1615 hours.

Nagato was beating on her keyboard. Her fingers were moving too fast to see, literally. It appeared that she didn't intend to waste any time on a bulky peripheral device such as a mouse. At some point Nagato had written her own macros for <The Day of Sagittarius 3> that allowed her to directly command her fleet through keyboard inputs. As a result the <Yuki Fleet> was battling as furiously as the great general Belisarius under Emperor Justinian's Byzantine Empire. However, she was seriously outnumbered.

We were only able to field three individual units—the <Yuki Fleet>, the <Koizumi Fleet>, and the <Kyon Fleet>—in battle, while the enemy had four fleets out and about, with the exception of <Dies Irae> (Enemy A). If there's one thing that history has taught us, it's this. Wars are won by numbers. If we're starting at a numerical disadvantage of three against four, our chances of enjoying a post-victory champagne fight are slim. Still, it wouldn't do to throw Haruhi and Asahina into the fray. That would only make it easier for our opponents to slaughter the entire armada in one fell swoop.

"The enemy appears to be using a vee formation in an attempt to draw us out."

Chief Officer Koizumi was whispering into my ear.

"The enemy formation is designed to trap us if we pursue. I would suggest we hold our positions and follow a defensive strategy."

Makes sense, sure. I'm fine with it, but what will Haruhi say? Besides.

I looked over Asahina's head to sneak a glance at Intelligence Officer Nagato's distinct profile.

I wasn't sure why. However, oddly enough, Nagato appeared to be asserting herself in a way I'd never seen before. Though the game had just started and her expression was neutral as always, the units of <Yuki Fleet> were already very active, moving around the screen and clearing operational objectives. What was it about <The Day of Sagittarius 3> that stirred Nagato's heart so?

Nagato hadn't been lying when she said that she was going to analyze this game. The alien artificial humanoid who could be classified as apathy incarnate knew every last detail about the computer society's original game. It was possible that she knew more about it than the people who actually made it. From her perspective, the computers found in modern Earth civilization might as well be a pre–Industrial Revolution relic from an assembly line. Using them was like twisting the arm of a baby.

Still, I had to wonder why the glint in Nagato's eyes had shifted from listless black to glittering silver.

Nagato was displaying extraordinary determination as she pounded away at the keyboard relentlessly as though this were a typing game. Her eyes were constantly darting around the screen, as she'd ditched the handy GUI for a small console in the corner of the screen. She typed in commands at finger-breaking speed.

"..."

The <Yuki Fleet> was constantly changing position and deploying scout vessels in a sweeping effort to locate the advancing enemy. Despite that, the only enemies located so far were <Enemy B> and <Enemy C>, the two fleets positioned right in front of our imperial armada. Nagato was engaged in a skirmish with those two fleets while holding the front line by herself. No time to stand around. Need to back her up.

And with that I set the <Kyon Fleet> into motion, which was when I suddenly found myself caught in a rain of beams from the side.

"The hell?" I blurted.

"Whoa there," Koizumi remarked.

I looked to see that his <Koizumi Fleet> was also being bombarded from the port side. <Enemy D> and <Enemy E> had practically come out of nowhere to flank Koizumi and me from both sides. The counter for the number of vessels in my <Kyon Fleet> was shrinking rapidly.

"What are you doing?!"

Haruhi yelled at me through her yellow megaphone.

"Fire back at them already! Counterattack!"

Don't need you to tell me that. These guys were clearly experienced enough to sneak past Nagato's network of scouts, but that didn't mean we were going to just lie down and surrender.

I ordered my <Kyon Fleet> to change directions and turn ninety degrees to starboard. Then I waited for the enemy to come into range of my weapons before opening fire with everything—but in that very moment <Enemy E> made a prompt U-turn and disappeared into the dark reaches of space. I was pretty pissed, so I sent a scout vessel in pursuit, but I wasn't able to find any trace of them.

"Damn, they got away."

It looked as if they were using a hit-and-run strategy with fleets that had their Speed parameters jacked up. <Enemy D>, which had been attacking the <Koizumi Fleet> from the starboard side, also disappeared with the same timing. I see. <B> and <C>, skirmishing with the <Yuki Fleet>, were merely a diversion while <D> and <E> were their main force. And their flagship fleet, <Enemy A>, was hiding somewhere and not even participating in the battle. That was their plan.

"Eep, I'm scared!"

Asahina had managed to clumsily send her own fleet into the corner of the screen. If she gets too far away from us, we'll lose our supply line and end up without any functioning weapons, but at this rate the battle will be finished before we even get a chance to worry about running out of energy or missiles. The <Computer Society Federation> has held the initiative the entire time.

After that, the flankers <Enemy D> and <Enemy E> continued to harass <Kyon Fleet> and <Koizumi Fleet> like stray dogs who keep returning around dinnertime after tasting leftovers once. If we tried to pursue, they would launch a bunch of homing missiles before escaping, which was a rather frustrating tactic that left us to flounder around. They were trying to whittle down our forces while avoiding a direct confrontation. Exactly what Haruhi hated the most.

Meanwhile, <Yuki Fleet> continued to advance alone by deftly eluding the wave of attacks from <Enemy B> and <Enemy C> while executing a probing counterattack with effective results. If it weren't for her fleet, the rest of us would be reduced to bits of interstellar matter floating in the void of space. Even if we lose, she deserves an award for bravery.

"…"

It looked like Nagato wasn't even breathing as she stared at her monitor. Her abuse of the keyboard didn't stop for a single moment. The computer society guys must have been surprised, since I was surprised myself.

Had to wonder if Haruhi's hatred of losing had spread to Nagato.

1630 hours.

We were bogged down in a stalemate now.

The computer society had realized that it would be difficult to deal with the vanguard <Yuki Fleet>, so <Enemy B> was left to focus on Nagato while the three other fleets, with the exception of their flagship fleet, <Enemy A>, whose whereabouts were still unknown, began attacking us from both sides alternately in interval waves. I had to be impressed by the level of coordination displayed by <C>, <D>, and <E>. When we turned our attention to <C>,

<D> would strike from the opposite side. Once we switched to pursue <D>, <E> would suddenly pop out from a third direction to fire its beams at us. This was about as much fun as playing a fighting game against an experienced pro who didn't know how to hold back. I would ask them to go easy on us, but there were multiple computers riding on this match.

However, the situation was considerably dire. As mentioned before, I'd put our chances of winning at less than 10 percent, but I still expected there to be a good show, at least. Fire at one another like crazy before exploding in a giant fireball, or the whole, "We lost but we put up a good fight so everything's okay" kind of thing.

But instead we have this painful battle of attrition.

"I can't take this any longer."

I suppose I should have seen this coming. Haruhi finally snapped and began to rattle off simple and clear orders to the flagship fleet under her command.

"All ships full speed ahead! Kyon, get out of my way! I'm going to find the enemy boss and beat him to a pulp!"

<Her Excellency☆Haruhi☆Fleet> attempted to cut between <Kyon Fleet> and <Koizumi Fleet>, but Koizumi and I moved together instantly like a school of small fish to stop her advance.

"What are you doing?! Koizumi, you're also going to interfere with my magnificent battle? Just get out of my way. I'll relieve you of your position as chief officer."

"That would be problematic."

Koizumi made no move to shift his fleet from its position blocking Haruhi's path.

"Your Excellency, please allow us to handle this. I, your humble servant, vow to protect Your Excellency until the moment I've drawn my last breath. You are free to dispose of me as you wish once the battle is over."

"Right."

I backed Koizumi up.

"If you want to improve our chances of winning, stay back. We haven't found the enemy flagship yet."

"So I'll go find him, then. He's probably somewhere around"— she pointed at the edge of her monitor, which we couldn't see—"here, so we'll head straight there. And then we fellow big-wigs will have it out mano a mano!"

I couldn't tell where she planned on heading, but <Her Excellency☆Haruhi☆Fleet> wouldn't have a chance to get there before she was torn apart like a beehive attacked by a bear about to go into hibernation.

Haruhi continued to push her fleet up as she thrust with the hand that was clutching her mouse.

"Nothing will change if we just sit around. I've been watching your pathetic attempts this whole time. Your <Kyon Fleet> keeps letting the enemy get away. And you've been losing forces in the process. Looks like I need to take charge."

"Could you stop that?"

I was busy using my fleet to block our flagship fleet's path while Koizumi happened to be doing the same thing on the other side. The three fleets from the <Computer Society Federation> may have noticed as they continued their successive hit-and-run attacks. Asahina had gotten her <Mikuru Fleet> completely lost in the void of space long ago.

"Where am I? Ah, I can't tell right from left now."

Asahina, sitting to my right, was close to tears as she looked between her screen and mine.

"Where did everyone go?"

Yes, I'm very sorry. Asahina, I can only say that you are free to wander wherever you please.

<Her Excellency☆Haruhi☆Fleet> was practically tailgating <Kyon Fleet>, so I couldn't move at all. Since I had essentially be-

come Haruhi's shield, the unrelenting enemy attack was whittling down the triangle that represented my unit.

"Outta the way!"

I couldn't even if I wanted to. The heartless <Koizumi Fleet> had made its withdrawal before Haruhi could rear-end him and was now exchanging fire with <Enemy D>, feigning ignorance. You're going to make me hold Haruhi back by myself?

"Damn."

I clicked the left mouse button furiously while moving the pointer around the screen randomly in an attempt to free my fleet from the <Her Excellency☆Haruhi☆Fleet>. The triangle for <Kyon Fleet> was noticeably smaller as it changed directions at the speed of a slug on a stroll. And during this time the enemy had a lock on my fleet and was firing beams and missiles like crazy.

We've lost.

I want to make it clear that I had no choice but to surrender at this point. With this girl as our commander, any chance of victory we'd had was long gone. An organization cannot operate smoothly without a composed leader at the top, and this applies to pretty much everything in life. I mean, I'm not entirely sure, but isn't that how it works?

As I bickered with Haruhi in both the real world and the virtual world, there was one SOS Brigade member with a firm grasp of the situation who stayed calm and continued playing the game.

—Or so I thought.

I finally realized this wasn't the case when I noticed the fingers of the brigade member sitting at the end of the table accelerating to a speed so fast that you'd have to record her with a high-sensitivity camera and play the footage back in slow motion to see what was going on.

It was Haruhi's duty and exclusive right to build up frustration to the point where she exploded. But this time, that didn't seem to be true.

The most excited person in the room at the moment was our SOS Brigade's knowledgeable intelligence officer and book-loving literary club member—

"…"

—Yuki Nagato.

1635 hours.

"Wha?"

I couldn't believe the sudden activity on my monitor as a foolish-sounding yelp escaped my lips.

"The hell is this?"

The forces of the <SOS Empire> now had a field of vision that was three times larger than it had been a moment ago. We could even see the current positions of the ever-elusive enemies <C>, <D>, and <E>. One was on the left wing taking aim at Koizumi's unit. One was in the process of turning around after making its escape. One was advancing on the entangled <Kyon Fleet> and <Her Excellency☆Haruhi☆Fleet>. Still, my focus was on the reason we were now able to see these enemy movements…

<Yuki Fleet> had split into twenty units.

"Well, well."

Koizumi's admiration sounded hollow to me.

"Nagato never ceases to amaze me. She actually picked up on this feature. I also considered using it at one point, but it was so complex that I abandoned the idea in the draft stage."

"Wait, Koizumi," I said. "Was this in the instruction manual?"

"It was. In the very back. I can teach you how it works. First, you press and hold the Ctrl key and F4 key while using the numpad to enter how many units you want to divide your fleet into—"

"No, that's enough. I'm not going to bother with it."

I looked back at the monitor.

The triangle corresponding to the <Yuki Fleet> had shriveled up like it'd been hit by some kind of shrink ray. Instead, I guess, there were twenty of those smaller triangles. I tried clicking one with the mouse pointer and the caption <Yuki Fleet 12> came up.

Micromanagement?

Of the little triangles numbered 01 through 20, some were continuing to exchange fire with <Enemy B>, some were threading the gaps in the enemy fleet to explore the unmapped area of space, and some had turned around to assist the hard-pressed <Kyon Fleet>.

Koizumi, explain this.

"Well, you see…We're allowed to divide our fleet into two or more groups and control them separately. Up to a maximum of twenty, I believe. That's what it said in the instruction manual."

"How does that help?"

"As you can see, our scouting capacity has improved significantly, since we've essentially added an additional twenty pairs of eyes. And there's more. For instance, by dividing your fleet into two groups, one can serve as a decoy while the other circles behind the enemy. However, the disadvantages trump the advantages, so the computer society chose not to employ this tactic."

Koizumi drew his face near mine as he whispered in a voice that Haruhi couldn't hear.

"This method requires one person to control multiple units. When you focus on one unit, the others are sitting around like wooden dolls. Thus, controlling twenty of these groups at the same time is beyond human ability."

I pictured the flabbergasted looks on the faces of the residents in the room next door as I looked to my side.

"Hey, Naga—"

The staccato beat of Nagato's pounding away at the keyboard

with her fingers had elevated from a noisy clatter…to a roaring rumble.

"U-um…If you hit it so hard, it'll break…"

Asahina offered a timid warning, but Nagato didn't even give her a glance. I followed her gaze to discover that there wasn't even a game window on her laptop screen. Instead there were a bunch of white characters on a black background, looking something like a BIOS setup menu on one of those ancient computers. And the text was scrolling by incredibly fast.

"Yes?"

Nagato didn't even look at me as she questioned my gaze.

"…Yeah."

Uh, Miss Nagato? What exactly might you be doing?

There was so much psychological pressure from the sight of Nagato beating away at the keyboard that my mental ramblings were forced to take a more respectful tone.

I took a quick glance at my own monitor to confirm that the twenty <Yuki Fleet> offspring were dancing around animatedly like tea stalks brought to life as they trifled with the enemy. There was no longer the issue of being unable to see the map…er, wait. I'm pretty sure I told you not to cheat.

"I am not."

Nagato murmured in a neutral tone. Then she finally turned to look at me for the first time, though her fingers never missed a beat.

"No special data manipulation is occurring. I am abiding by the set rules."

Asahina was leaning her small frame back in an apparent attempt to avoid Nagato's gaze. Nagato continued to stare into my eyes.

"I have not taken any action that is not allowed by this simulation program."

"R-really? Sorry about that, then."

I could sense this terrifying aura emanating from her short hair.

However, the expression on Nagato's face was as inorganic as always, so I was expecting her usual "Yes" followed by utter silence, but this time she continued speaking.

An indictment of the enemy.

"The actions of the computer society are what would be considered cheating."

At that moment Haruhi managed to successfully disengage her units from the units of <Kyon Fleet>.

"So slow! Why am I slow? Will it speed up if I pour an energy drink on the computer?"

It was clear that she was engrossed in jaunting up to the front lines with her fleet.

I leaned over Asahina to whisper my question to Nagato.

"What do you mean when you say that they're cheating?"

Nagato didn't let up on her high-speed blind typing for a second as she gave her detached reply.

"They are utilizing commands that do not exist on our computers, which afford them an advantage in this simulated space battle."

"What do you mean?"

Nagato fell silent for a moment and blinked as though she were collecting her thoughts.

"Their fog of war is off."

A murmur that was elaborated on in the same soft tone.

According to her explanation, the "fog of war" had been turned off for the computer society at the beginning of the game. Naturally, there was no such convenient option in our version. I don't even know what the difference would be, though. What does this mean?

"With the fog of war on, players are obligated to scout the map.

When the fog of war is off, that is no longer required. They have minimized their scouting efforts as they have become unnecessary."

Uh, so what does that even mean?

"With the fog of war off, all areas of the map are illuminated."

Meaning...

"The entire map, including our positions, was visible from the beginning."

That was easy to understand, for a Nagato explanation.

"That is not all."

The stony-faced alien-made life-form continued her spiel in an indifferent voice.

Based on what she said, the <Computer Society Federation> fleets were equipped with a warp function. That would explain how they were able to pop up at the perfect time. They had a five-hundred-year jump on the <SOS Empire> in terms of technology. It'd be like pitting infantry from the Warring States period against the Japan Ground Self-Defense Force 7th Division. We never had a chance to win, huh?

"Yes."

Nagato confirmed my suspicion.

"Defeat was our only option."

Was, huh? Past tense. So? What about now? I was hoping that she'd reiterate that sentence in the present tense, but the sight of faint emotion stirring in Nagato's black eyes for the first time ever left me scratching my head a bit.

"But you know, Nagato. I would prefer that you don't use your alien powers. I understand that they pulled a fast one on us. Still, if we use that as a reason to use further bogus magic, that'll make us no better than them. No, we'd be below them. Since your tricks break the physical laws of this planet."

"I am not disobeying your instructions."

Nagato's reply came instantly.

"I only wish to apply alterations to the program that conform to the current level of technology on Earth. No modifications will be made to the union of data in known space. Countermeasures will be implemented against the computer society. Permission?"

Are you talking to me?

"You are the one who set restrictions on my data-processing capabilities."

…

It's been half a year since we first met. I don't mean to brag, but over the past six months I've become competent enough to pick up on the slight emotional changes—assuming that she's even capable of feeling emotion—behind that taciturn mask of hers. Right now, Nagato's pale face was clearly showing a picogram's worth of determination.

Asahina was gaping at me in surprise. Koizumi's eyes were also on me, but he had a wry smile on his face. Haruhi was the only one yelling by herself while unloading her beams and missiles. At this rate she would run out of ammunition in the middle of the enemy formation. There wasn't much time left for me to make up my mind.

How do I respond?… That question only required a few seconds of deliberation. Nagato was eager to do this. This was the first time I'd ever seen her like this. I couldn't help but feel that this was a good sign. An organic android created by the Data Overmind that was identical in every way to an ordinary human. It was possible that she'd developed the cliché robot desire to become a human.

And I didn't see any problem with that.

"Okay, Nagato. Go for it."

I gave her a smile of encouragement as I issued my figurative seal of approval.

"You're free to do whatever you want, as long as it's within human capability. Deal the computer society a crushing blow. End this the way Haruhi would want, so they never come back to complain again."

Nagato stared at me for a long time. At least, it felt like a long time to me.

"Yes."

And with that exceedingly short response, Nagato hit the Enter key and just like that, the tables were instantly turned.

1647 hours.

A cunning trap had already been placed.

I was left dumbfounded by how abruptly everything was happening, which only served to show that my capacity for surprise was on the same level as that of little boys, training to be monks, who were still wet behind the ears. Our opponents from the computer society were probably panicking like Wall Street on the second day of the Great Depression.

Everything came as a result of Nagato's micromanagement technique. Good thing she's on our side. I should probably make her an offering or two out of my own pocket. If I happen to see a book that looks interesting, I'll buy it for her as a present. Come to think of it, when would her birthday even be?

Well, I can think about that stuff later. For now, I'll return to my commentary on the current situation.

The enemy fleets had stopped in their tracks in a virtual visualization of the confusion the opposing players felt.

Nagato had used her laptop to hack into the five computers of the computer society and directly tweak the program they were running. Don't ask me how she did it. I wouldn't know. In any case, her objective was to turn on our opponents' fog of war. As a result, the <Computer Society Federation> had its visibility reduced significantly. Its screens would be a lot darker now, since it never had any need to send out scout vessels, and in fact hadn't done so, according to our intelligence officer.

Nagato had also rewritten the source code for <Computer Society Federation>'s program so its fog of war would be locked in the "on" setting and added a layer of protection that prevented anyone else from changing the code again. However, she didn't delete its warp function. Instead, she made some slight adjustments and left it intact. Part of the scheme Nagato had devised.

All of this was done while she deftly micromanaged twenty separate groups without the assistance of any alien powers, so the fact that she was under the constraints of an ordinary human didn't stop her from putting on a phenomenal performance.

"Well, our chance has finally come."

Koizumi smiled cheerfully as he narrated the situation on the screen.

"Take a look. <Enemy C> and <Enemy D> have lost sight of our position because of the interference from the numerous divisions of <Yuki Fleet>. <Enemy E> is currently engaged in battle with me, and <Enemy B> will soon be in range of <Her Excellency☆Haruhi☆Fleet>."

"Enemy found!"

Haruhi shouted with glee to confirm Koizumi's commentary.

"Fire! Fire! Fire!"

Haruhi nearly banged her forehead on the monitor as she bellowed.

The liberated <Her Excellency☆Haruhi☆Fleet> launched a barrage of beams and missiles in every direction as she rushed toward the enemy fleet. The befuddled <Enemy B> quickly turned to escape, but my <Kyon Fleet> was already waiting for him on the other side.

"Here you go."

One slight motion by my finger sent all my beams shooting into the nose of <Enemy B>.

"Hey, Kyon! Those are mine! Let me have them!"

The formation of the surrounded <Enemy B> instantly fell apart. The quivering <Enemy B> unit indicator eventually blew up with a small beep. One down.

Haruhi set off in search of another target as she moved her fleet, the mobile fireworks dispenser, to <Enemy E>'s flank next. <Enemy E> was already engaged with Koizumi and the addition of a second fleet to deal with led to its numbers' being whittled down quickly.

With the situation quickly worsening, <Enemy E> must have decided that he was out of options. He finally resorted to using their secret command in plain sight of <SOS Empire> forces for the first time in this match.

"Ah, he disappeared! Huh? How?"

Haruhi cried out and I knew that it was finally time. <Enemy E> vanished from its previous position in space, which was in the middle of a crossfire.

Must be that warp thing. They should have come up with a better name. "Warp" is such an outdated term.

However, this was the core of Nagato's crafty trap.

"Huh? Something else is appearing."

I listened to the sound of Haruhi's voice, as I'd already stopped.

"Eek?!"

An adorable-sounding shriek escaped Asahina as she blinked at the monitor.

"Kyon, the one I was controlling just went off somewhere…"

<Enemy E> wasn't the only one to warp. The <Her Excellency☆Haruhi☆Fleet> was left alone while every vessel, friend and foe, was teleported through space.

Nagato had altered the program so that when a computer society fleet activated the warp function, all units on both sides, with the exception of the <Her Excellency☆Haruhi☆Fleet>, would be simultaneously entered in a compulsory warp that sent each fleet to a designated position on the map.

An eye for an eye, a cheat for a cheat. As long as you don't go overboard.

The shock being experienced next door would put the jolt from the fog of war's being turned on to shame. For the first time I was able to see the computer society flagship fleet, <Enemy A> (Dies something), on the screen. Once I saw his position, I had to shrug.

"Karma's a bitch."

The president's <Enemy A> was directly in front of the <Her Excellency☆Haruhi☆Fleet>.

Behind him at point-blank range was the unscathed <Mikuru Fleet>, which had been transported in a similar fashion. The <Koizumi Fleet> had taken a short warp to secure his starboard side while the <Yuki Fleet> had regrouped to handle the port side. The significantly smaller <Kyon Fleet> was standing by to the side. I looked to see where the other computer society members were, to discover that the other four fleets had been transported to the corners of the vast map. They won't be able to make it back in time.

The full armada of the <SOS Empire> had the sole fleet of <Enemy A> completely surrounded.

"I don't really get it."

Haruhi smacked her lips as she waved an arm in the air.

"All ships fire everything you have! Let the enemy commander taste hellfire!"

And with that signal Haruhi, Koizumi, Nagato, and I all simultaneously fired every weapon in our fleets. Asahina, who started to tremble upon hearing Nagato say "Fire" in a cold voice, also made her first strike of the day as she joined in bombarding the completely surrounded <Enemy A>.

"I'm sorry…" Asahina murmured.

The computer society president was the one who had absolutely no idea what was going on. Since he'd been sitting in the back and watching the show when their fog of war cheat was disabled and he was suddenly warped into the middle of the enemy formation without ever touching a button.

"Good…"

Grief. I swallowed that last word. Koizumi smirked at me. I ignored him.

I turned my attention back to the screen to find that the president's <Enemy A> fleet was squirming like an upside-down turtle as he was hit by a shower of short-range beams and a rain of missiles. Well, he deserved it this time. They were the ones who decided that they weren't going to make things fair. Still, we can't really criticize them when we have Yuki Nagato, whose very existence is unfair.

Nagato never let up on her rapid input of weapon fire commands until the very end. The <Enemy A> fleet unit counter was dropping as fast as the remaining ammo counter on an M61 Vulcan. The last remaining unit was taken out by a perfect snipe from the <Yuki Fleet> that was accurate to the last pixel, and that was the end of the enemy flagship.

A simple fanfare began to play as flashing words appeared on all five monitors to signal that the game was over.

YOU WIN!

1501 hours.

Ten minutes after the battle was concluded, someone knocked on the clubroom door.

The computer society members came staggering in, including the president, who was noticeably subdued.

"You got us. We were completely defeated. I'll admit it. My

apologies. I'm sorry. Please forgive us. We bow before you. We underestimated you. We were wrong. We were utterly destroyed."

The president had his head bowed down in front of Haruhi as she looked down on him like he was a sundial. The members of the computer society were pale and visibly shaken as they endured Her Excellency Haruhi's stern glare.

"I never would have thought that you'd be able to see through our trick so easily...I can't deny that we used some underhanded methods. But still...I never expected someone to rewrite the game code while we were playing...Hard to believe...but it actually happened..."

The president was glancing around the room as though he were in a world of make-believe. Haruhi raised one eyebrow.

"What are you mumbling about? I don't want to hear any excuses about why you lost. So, you remember your promise, right?"

She cheerfully wagged a finger in front of the president's face. She was so happy about winning that she didn't even care to question the bizarre way we won. As far as she was concerned, a win was a win.

"No more complaints, right? This computer belongs to me, and those laptops also belong to us. I won't let you say that you forgot. If you do, I'll make your life a living hell. Yes, I'll start by penalizing you with ten laps around the grounds in the nude while screaming at the top of your lungs that you're being chased by little green men."

Haruhi's outrageous babbling only served to make the computer society bunch hang their heads lower. Asahina stepped in, either out of pity or because she couldn't bear the tension in the room.

"Ah...yes. Would you like some tea?"

The ever-considerate Asahina stood up and headed for the kettle. Koizumi looked amused as he took out a pack of paper cups from a pile of assorted crap. Nagato remained seated in her metal chair as she stared with humorless eyes at the subdued male students lined up in front of Haruhi.

Haruhi was giving some kind of impassioned speech when one of the members, the president, drifted over to me.

"Say," he said in a thin voice. "Who was responsible for that feat? The amazing superhacker who could probably crack anything in the world? ...Well, I can guess who it was..."

Nagato slowly looked up at me while the president looked at her.

Pretty obvious. An outsider could still tell that Nagato was the most likely candidate when brains were involved.

"I have a proposition."

The president turned to Nagato.

"If you ever happen to have free time, would you be interested in participating in computer society activities? I mean, could you please?"

And now the guy's trying to solicit her. Just a moment earlier, his eyes had been as dead as the eyes of a frozen Pacific saury that had been left under the sun for three days, and now they were full of life. Once a human hits rock bottom, his only choice is to fight back.

Nagato turned her face to the president before turning back to me with a slow, mechanical motion. She said nothing as she stared at me with a questioning glint in her dark glassy eyes.

"..."

What is this? Is she trying to communicate with me through telepathy? Or does she want me to make the decision for her? You can't just give me a look (blank as it may be) and expect me to solve everything. The question was for you. You can make up your own mind. In fact, that's what you're supposed to do.

I followed Nagato's lead as I attempted to silently beam my response to her.

"Hey, hey. What do you think you're doing?"

Haruhi walked over to butt in.

"You don't get to rent Yuki without my permission. Talk to me first."

Uncanny hearing. She was actually listening to our conversation. Haruhi placed her hands on her hips as she struck a haughty pose that deserved commendation.

"Understood? She's the SOS Brigade's indispensable reticent character. I saw her first. You're too late. She won't be going any-where!"

I'm pretty sure that you wanted the clubroom, not Nagato.

"Doesn't matter! Yuki came with the clubroom. I refuse to give up anything in this room, even if it's a can of soda without any fizz."

Haruhi puffed up her sailor uniform–clad chest as she laid claim to everything in the room.

"Just hold on a sec."

I interrupted Haruhi before pausing to think.

I considered myself to be a better judge of Nagato's expressions than anybody else out there. After all, I actually met Nagato three years ago. True, she was able to completely avoid showing any emotion on her face, but I had come to realize that she still had feelings. There was that summer vacation in loop mode, and this game made it clear. Yes, just like that one time way back when I took her to the public library.

There had to be something out there that interested Nagato.

In fact, Nagato had been the most passionate one in our <The Day of Sagittarius 3> battle with the computer society, not Haruhi. She looked more enthusiastic when she was punching away at the keyboard than when she was reading books. I wasn't sure if this was related to my ban on dirty tricks. Either way, it looked to me like she was somehow having fun as she pounded away at the keyboard. If she'd managed to find a new hobby to go along with reading difficult books, why stand in her way? It would be more gratifying for her to interact with other people and adapt to life at this school instead of sitting in the SOS Brigade hideout like a piece of furniture.

I'm sure that even Nagato would get tired of observing Haruhi all the time. An alien-made organic humanoid interface would still go for some recreation every now and then.

"Do what you want."

Just this once, I took the president's side.

"Did you enjoy playing with computers? In that case, you can go next door whenever you feel like playing with their computers. They'd probably appreciate it if you debugged their homemade games or something. They probably have better toys than the ones here."

Nagato didn't say anything, but I could notice a micron of movement in the expression on her face as she stared at me. She seemed to be seeking permission and guidance at the same time. I could sense a flicker of hesitation pass over Nagato's black, candylike eyes.

It felt like she was taking forever, but in reality, it only took her as long as three blinks of the eye.

"…Yes."

I didn't get a chance to ask what she was saying yes to before Nagato nodded stiffly and looked up at the president before speaking in that same neutral tone.

"Every now and then."

Haruhi was sulking, naturally.

"We were the ones who won, so why do I have to rent out one of my precious brigade members? This is going to cost you. Yes, a thousand yen per minute as a bare minimum."

I'd be willing to pay a thousand yen a minute.

"Your Excellency."

Koizumi had apparently finished his tea as he walked over with that trademark smile of his.

"A person of your station must on occasion afford the vanquished tribute for their efforts. A leader must not only be strong, but demonstrate that she can be magnanimous."

"Huh? Really?"

Haruhi puckered her lips like a duckbill.

"Well, if Yuki's okay with it...But! I'm not giving back the laptops. Oh, one more thing."

She had apparently come up with a brilliant idea while she was talking. Haruhi shot the president a glare before smirking. Her face was certainly busy.

"Listen up. You people are the losers. You have to do whatever the victors tell you to do. This is war."

She snatched a cup of tea (Karigane, was it?) from the tray Asahina had quietly brought over and gulped it down before continuing.

"All of you must pledge absolute fealty to me. Yep, I won't treat you badly. I'm a fan of meritocracy. Depending on your performance, I may promote you to full brigade members. For instance...yes, I'll work you hard when we declare all-out war on the student council. Until then, you'll be junior brigade members."

Don't tell me that she's planning on recruiting the entire student body into the SOS Brigade. However, Haruhi was too elated to pay any heed to my fears.

"Koizumi, prepare the treaty at once."

"By your command, Your Excellency."

Koizumi smiled like a custodial minister manipulating a young emperor before he began typing away on his newly acquired laptop.

*　　　*　　　*

The clubroom didn't see much change over the next few days, just the addition of a few laptops that were completely wasted on us. Asahina was tidying up the place in her maid outfit while boiling water in the kettle on the portable gas stove. Koizumi was playing backgammon by himself. Nagato sat at the corner of the table reading. A brief moment of peace before Haruhi told us her next brilliant scheme.

As we savored this constant everyday SOS Brigade period after school, the book-loving alien would be absent on rare occasion. A few minutes after I noticed she was missing, she would pop back up and start reading again. As far as I was concerned, Nagato was the true master of this clubroom.

"…"

As I watched Nagato read a foreign mystery novel, I couldn't notice anything different about her on the outside. On the inside…well, I wouldn't know that.

Nagato was here, just as always. She would drift next door from time to time like a fickle breeze. That was enough.

"Kyon, here you go. I tried making Chinese tea this time. Hee hee…how is it?"

I accepted my personal teacup from the demurely smiling Asahina and slowly savored the tea, but my taste buds were unable to discern any difference from the other tea leaves she used before. She could serve wheatgrass juice and it would taste heavenly.

As I searched my vocabulary for the right words to express my thoughts to the eagerly waiting Asahina, I came to the conclusion that nothing weird would be happening for a while.

I wouldn't realize how wrong that prediction was until a month later, halfway through December, with winter vacation and Christmas right around the corner.

It all became clear once Haruhi mysteriously disappeared.

PREFACE · WINTER

A whole plethora of words come to mind when discussing Haruhi Suzumiya, naturally, but if I had to describe her in a single sentence, it would go something like the following.

Here we have the last person in Japan who should be allowed near the launch mechanism of a nuclear missile.

Though common sense dictated that an ordinary girl in high school had virtually no chance of ever gaining access to such an item, we were dealing with a girl who defied the highest of exponential odds. Any outcome was possible when she was in the mix. However, despite the fact that she was a loose cannon on a level that was far more ruinous than that of a time bomb without a countdown or a nuclear reactor that was guaranteed to experience a meltdown, it wasn't necessary to disable her completely, as the implementation of a "pause mode" would suffice to make her manageable, a lesson that I finally learned after enduring a significant amount of agony.

Long story short, we simply had to prevent her from getting bored and she wouldn't bother with stuff like nuclear missiles. We simply had to redirect her enthusiasm to something else for brief periods of time, much as I would toss the cap of a plastic bottle to our calico Shamisen so he could nibble on it for three minutes or so, though we would need to devote a great deal of energy to finding that something else for her to focus on—

That more or less summarized the reasoning Koizumi had asserted way back when. And he still subscribed to that line of thought.

Which was why we found ourselves in another ridiculous predicament.

Predicament? Yes, I kid you not. Predicament with a capital "P." I doubt you'd be able to find a more appropriate situation to apply that word to.

For at the moment we were absolutely, positively, and completely stranded.

SNOWY MOUNTAIN SYNDROME

"We're screwed."

Haruhi gave a rather frank assessment of our current situation as she walked ahead of me.

"Can't see a thing."

You want to know where we are? We went to a remote island during summer vacation. Now guess where Haruhi would want to go over winter vacation.

"That's odd."

I could hear Koizumi's voice from his position at the end of our group.

"My sense of distance tells me that we should have reached the foot of the mountain a while ago."

Here's a hint. We're in a cold and white place.

"I'm freezing…brr."

The howling wind made it difficult to catch her words. I looked behind me to confirm that the girl in skiwear was waddling along like a duckling. I gave her a nod of encouragement before turning back to the front.

"…"

I got the feeling that Nagato's strides were growing heavier as she led the way. White crystal snow was sticking to our ski boots so that more accumulated with every step taken. Where would such a phenomenon occur?

This is too much effort. I'll just give you the answer.

An expanse of white as far as the eye can see with icy snow in every direction.

Yes, we were clearly on a snowy mountain.

We'd arrived at a ski lodge in the middle of a blizzard, and now we were stranded on this snowy mountain—that would be the most accurate description of our current situation.

Now then. Who arranged for this scenario? For once, I was hoping that this whole mess was scripted. Otherwise the five of us would simply freeze to death and our frozen corpses wouldn't be discovered until spring, when the snow melted.

Koizumi, deal with this.

"Easier said than done."

Koizumi looked down at his compass.

"We should be going in the right direction. Nagato's navigation is impeccable. Yet we've been unable to find our way off this mountain after trudging through the snow for hours. Completely unthinkable under normal circumstances, wouldn't you say?"

So what's going on here? We're never getting out of this?

"I am positive that unnatural forces are at work here. There was no way to predict this happening. Nagato doesn't know the cause either. After all, we only know that this was entirely unexpected."

I can figure that out for myself. If we can't find our way back with Nagato in the lead, something's definitely wrong.

Again? Did Haruhi have another one of her worthless ideas?

"That is not a certainty at the moment. I have a hunch that Suzumiya would never desire the occurrence of such a phenomenon."

How can you be so sure?

"After all, Suzumiya was looking forward to a murder mystery drama playing out at the mountain lodge. I had everything planned out to accommodate her expectations."

There was a "murder game" planned for this winter ski trip, as a follow-up to the one the preceding summer. The previous attempt had been more along the lines of a prank that failed, while this time we were simply playing detective with everyone knowing beforehand that the crime was staged. In fact, the cast from the first take had made a reappearance, with Arakawa the butler, Mori the maid, and the Tamaru brothers acting in the same roles as before.

"You have a point…"

I mean, Haruhi was dying to identify the killer and reveal her brilliant deduction, so she wouldn't subconsciously wish for something to happen that night that would prevent us from returning to the lodge.

On top of that, Tsuruya and my sister, who served as temporary extras on occasion, along with Shamisen, were waiting for us to return.

Truth be told, the lodge we were staying at belonged to the Tsuruya family. That bright and cheerful young lady offered to provide lodging on the condition that she could tag along. Shamisen was needed as a prop for the scheme Koizumi had cooked up, and my sister attached herself to my luggage. The pair of girls plus one animal weren't part of the motley crew stranded out here. Shamisen was probably curled up in front of the fireplace while Tsuruya was keeping my skiing-impaired sister company building snowmen. That was the last I had seen of them.

The three of them were essentially junior SOS Brigade members, as far as Haruhi was concerned. There was no reason for any of us to be against the idea of seeing them again, and that went double for Haruhi.

So why? Why weren't we able to return to the heated lodge that was serving as the SOS Brigade winter vacation site?

If Nagato's powers weren't enough to get us to our destination, what was going on here?

"We ran into a hurricane last summer, and now we have a blizzard…"

Was there some kind of rule that stated that we were required to encounter logic-defying phenomena every time our school had an extended period of vacation?

I was feeling a mix of doubt and unease as I recalled our past adventures.

"Why did things turn out this way?"

That would be the cue to switch to flashback mode.

………

……

…

It was more or less inevitable that we would go on a trip during winter vacation. I mean, we wouldn't have been any less surprised by its happening if we had somehow been able to see the future.

After all, it had been loudly announced on the ferry ride back from the remote island murder tour (hurricane included), which had started on the first day of summer vacation. By whom? Who else but Haruhi. The rest of us had no choice but to accept her declaration, while Koizumi was named the tour guide.

I'd been hoping that Haruhi might find something else more interesting by the time winter came around, but our brigade chief apparently had an excellent memory when it came to having fun.

"Counting down to the new year in a blizzard."

Haruhi distributed a number of stapled papers before grinning at us the way a kidnapper would at a child.

"We'll be going to a snow lodge this winter, just as planned. Part two of our magical mystery tour!"

This was taking place in the clubroom on the twenty-fourth, right after the closing ceremony. A bubbling ceramic pot sat atop the portable gas stove that was sitting on the long table as we tossed an assortment of ingredients into the pot to serve as our lunch.

Haruhi was adding meat, fish, and vegetables in the wrong order while Asahina the maid, with a scarf around her head, was using a pair of long chopsticks to dish out the food after letting it drain a bit. The rest of the SOS Brigade, Nagato, Koizumi, and I, simply ate, and we were joined by a special guest today.

"Whoa, good stuff! What is this? *Munch*…is Harls a chef prodigy? *Chomp*…whew. The broth is exquisite. *Slurp*."

It was Tsuruya. The owner of that cheerful voice was in a virtual eating contest with Nagato the silent connoisseur as she exclaimed with glee at intervals while using her chopsticks to rapidly scoop food from the pot to her plate.

"A hot pot really hits the spot when it's winter! And it was a riot to see Kyon in that reindeer getup. Man, this day has been a blast!"

You were the only person to appreciate that act, Tsuruya. Haruhi and Koizumi were smirking at me the entire time, while Asahina had covered her face halfway through and started to shake with mirth. Nagato was clearly wondering where the humor was, an exceedingly logical response. Honestly, the experience was so nerveracking that I was dripping cold sweat the entire time. I clearly lacked the necessary talent for making people laugh. Not that I ever had any intention to become an entertainer, but whatever.

Tsuruya wasn't here as part of the hot pot spectacle or to chaperone Asahina. As for why she was our special guest today…

"So about that snowstorm lodge."

Haruhi had upgraded the modifier from "snow" to "snowstorm."

"Rejoice, Kyon. Guess what? Tsuruya is letting us use her vacation home for free. I hear that the location's fantastic. Can't wait to see it! Here, chow down."

Haruhi tossed a chunk of pork onto Tsuruya's plate and dropped a piece of fish that had finished cooking onto her own plate.

"I usually go with my family."

Tsuruya threw the chunk of pork into her mouth and swallowed it whole.

"But this year the 'rents are in Europe on a business trip. They'll be finished in three days and the whole family will be going to Switzerland to ski afterward! So I'll take you guys to the vacation home with me! Sounds like it'll be a blast!"

Tsuruya must have heard Asahina mention Haruhi's winter plans at some point and offered to provide lodging. Koizumi was probably standing by to jump at the first opportunity presented, so he wrote up a vacation plan and presented it to Haruhi, who jumped with joy like a cat receiving sashimi.

"I've got something here for Tsuruya!"

She withdrew a plain armband from her desk and labeled it HONORARY ADVISOR before handing it over. Right.

Speaking of Koizumi, he was smiling as he watched Haruhi, Nagato, and Tsuruya dig in like this was some kind of eating contest before he apparently noticed the look on my face.

"Please rest assured. There won't be any surprises this time. Everyone will be aware that we are merely playing a game of detective. In fact, we will be using the same members as before."

Arrangements had been made for Arakawa the butler, Mori the maid, and the Tamaru brothers to put on another show for us. I guess that works, but what do those people even do for a living? Are they desk jockeys at your "Agency" thing?

"They are all actors I happen to be acquainted with from a small troupe... Would that satisfy your curiosity?"

If Haruhi's willing to accept that story, I'll take it.

"Suzumiya does not concern herself with the details as long as she is having fun, though the provision of entertainment would be the greatest hurdle before us...My stomach begins to hurt when I worry if my script will be to her liking."

Koizumi clutched at his stomach in an exaggerated gesture, but the smile on his face made it clear that he wasn't even trying to act like he was in pain.

I believed myself to be a better human than Haruhi, so I couldn't ignore reality the way she did and party away without a concern. I glanced around the room for something that might alleviate my worries before spotting Nagato and the blank look on her face. Your typical Nagato. The Nagato I was accustomed to was chomping away at the hot pot as if nothing had ever happened.

"..."

In any case, I thought.

For once, we should prevent the situation from deteriorating to a point where any strain would be placed on Nagato. No, we were obligated to do so. Though experience would tell us that we should be safe this time. Nagato hadn't been required to perform any spectacular feats during our summer camp. I could only hope that this winter trip would be the same. Leave the hard work to Koizumi and his people.

As I considered this, I looked down at the documents before me.

According to the schedule on these sheets of paper, our departure was set for December thirtieth. The day before New Year's Eve. The snowy mountain itself wasn't that far away. A few hours of bumpy train riding would get us there on the same day.

In any case, once we arrived the rest of that day would be spent skiing, followed by a party (no alcohol allowed) that night. The arrangements for food preparation were similar to those on the summer island, as Arakawa the butler (who was more convincing than a real butler, despite being a fake) and Sonoh Mori (the fake maid) were in charge. The two Tamaru brothers would arrive the next morning, which would lead us to the prelude of our little detective game.

We would spend New Year's Eve analyzing the case and deducing the trick behind it before assembling at midnight to present our individual theories concerning the "Poisoned Chocolate Incident," with Koizumi playing the role of the mastermind who would reveal the solution in a nonchalant manner. And then we would all be filled with this sense of relief as we bid farewell to the old year and welcomed the new. Glad to see you!

At least, that was the plan.

I looked up to see Haruhi practically beaming at me. I'm no longer surprised by her ability to gloat before she's actually accomplished anything.

"We'll ring in the new year with a bang."

Haruhi was in the process of snatching up a leek with her chopsticks.

"I'm sure that the new year will appreciate our efforts and make this year a good one. I guarantee it. I can sense that the upcoming year will be a turning point for the SOS Brigade."

I don't really care about your personifying years, but I doubt that your definition of a good year would be good for the rest of us.

"Really? I was thinking that the past year was a lot of fun and hoping that next year would be the same. You don't agree? Oh, Mikuru. The broth in the hot pot's boiling down, so add some more water."

"Ah, right away."

Asahina pranced over to the kettle.

"Oof."

She heaved the heavy-looking kettle above the hot pot and carefully tipped it over.

As I watched her graceful movements, I reflected on everything that had happened in the past year, which made me hesitate for a moment. Haruhi had said that the past year was a lot of fun. If you were to ask me if I thought the past year was fun, my answer would be obvious.

After all, I'd started off as a kid who longed for the mysterious and unknown. I just wanted an experience that involved aliens or anything along those lines. It wouldn't make sense for me to not be happy about my fantasies' becoming reality. Still, I wouldn't expect such events to continue regularly.

However, despite all that, this was how I felt on the inside.

Yeah, it was fun.

I could confidently say that now. It took a considerable amount of time for me to reach this point. But to be completely honest, I would have preferred a little more peace and quiet. Personally, a few more intervals of relaxation in the clubroom would have been nice.

"You say such weird things."

Haruhi's cheeks were stuffed with fish liver.

"We've been having a blast this whole time. You haven't had enough fun yet? Then we should party hard before the year ends."

"That won't be necessary."

She didn't know about the ordeals I'd experienced and how I'd managed to survive them. I'd had to win a baseball game, end summer vacation, restore the distortions to reality that had come from the movie, go back and forth between past and present, and establish the fact that I will need to return to the past again in the future. The choice had been my own, so I couldn't blame anybody else, but I was ridiculously busy this time of year for somebody who wasn't planning on becoming a teacher.

Well, not that I could say any of this to Haruhi.

"We'll have time to party after we get to that mountain lodge."

I brushed aside Haruhi's extended chopsticks as I plucked some cabbage from the hot pot. It wasn't every day you got a chance to have some of Haruhi's special hot pot. I needed to fill my stomach before the females of the group (excluding Asahina) with their voracious appetites devoured all the food. Didn't know when I'd get another chance to enjoy such a feast.

"I guess."

Haruhi was in a good humor as she heaped beef tripe onto her own plate.

"We need to light up the place with our partying. Got it? New Year's Eve only happens once a year. Just think about it. We only get to experience a certain day of a certain year once in our lifetime. The same goes for today. Today will never come back once it's gone. That's why you're obligated to live every day to the fullest so you have no regrets. I'm determined to make every single day of my life unforgettable."

Haruhi's idealistic sermon drew a quick response from the adjacent Tsuruya, who was sinking her teeth into some half-cooked chicken.

"Wow. Harls, you can remember everything that happened 365 days a year? Wowzers. Mikuru, give me some tea!"

"Ah, right away!"

Asahina held the teapot in one hand as she carefully poured green tea into the guest teacup Tsuruya was holding up, looking rather happy as she performed the task. Haruhi was having fun arbitrarily administering the hot pot, Koizumi had a rather elegant smile on his face as the steam emitted from the hot pot, and Nagato simply dug in without making a sound. Tsuruya, the honorary advisor, was here as a temporary brigade member, but for the most part this was your typical SOS Brigade atmosphere.

I now understood the true value of these brief moments we shared. Having chosen this world, I was more or less guaranteed to encounter more bizarre happenings that involved Haruhi. At the very least, I'd expect to run into a couple more of these before everything was said and done.

Besides, we haven't come across any sliders yet.

"If you plan on making an appearance, just bring it."

I accidentally said that out loud, but apparently nobody could hear me over the ruckus of Haruhi and Tsuruya fighting over mushrooms.

However, I have a feeling that Nagato's eyelashes twitched ever so slightly.

I glanced over at the window to see that snow was trickling down slowly, as if against the sky's will. Koizumi must have followed my gaze.

"Once you reach our destination, you'll have enough snow to play with until you're sick of it. Incidentally, do you prefer skiing or snowboarding? I happen to be in charge of arranging for the implements we will use."

"Never snowboarded before."

I tossed him a halfhearted reply as I looked away from the winter sky. Koizumi still had that neutral smile on his face, though it seemed a bit forced.

"Now then, are you staring at the falling snow or thinking of a certain girl whose name happens to mean 'snow' in another language…"

It was clear that there was nothing to gain from exchanging glances with Koizumi. I shrugged and joined the battle for mushrooms.

We got away with the forbidden gas stove without being discovered by any teachers or tattletale students, though it was possible they noticed and chose to ignore us. Either way, we ate until we were stuffed, cleaned up the pot, utensils, and trash, and left the clubroom. By the time we exited the school building the light snow had stopped.

After bidding farewell to Tsuruya, who had to attend a party at her home, the SOS Brigade members headed to the bakery. Once we picked up the extra-large cake Haruhi had ordered, we set off to Nagato's apartment.

Not because we felt bad about Nagato spending Christmas Eve all by herself, but because Nagato, who lived alone, had offered the ideal place for eating cake and going wild. I couldn't be sure if Koizumi, tasked with bringing Twister, or I, carrying the cake box, got the better deal, but Haruhi was clearly in a joyous mood as she skipped ahead of our little group. Her cheer had apparently spread to Asahina, whom Haruhi would swing around from time to time, and Nagato, who silently shuffled along.

It seemed that we wouldn't have to worry about a blizzard of Santa Clauses instead of snow. Haruhi certainly appeared to be satisfied as she enjoyed this very ordinary Christmas Eve. She was in the same mental state as my sister. Just for today though, probably.

I shouldn't need to explain the reason I was feeling so tolerant this time of year. Haruhi could suddenly propose that we go Santa hunting and roam the night streets, and I would simply join her with a mocking smile on my face.

It was undeniably true that every one of us appeared to be having fun as we played the various games Koizumi had brought to Nagato's soundproof room. Two laptops were hooked up for a <The Day of Sagittarius 3> tournament that was dominated by Nagato. I found myself jostling with Haruhi in a game of Twister. It was such a crazy night that we were on the verge of inviting in random couples who happened to be passing by—

And that was essentially how our Christmas Eve went.

*   *   *

The period between Christmas Eve and New Year's Eve flew by so fast that I had to wonder if Haruhi was pushing time along. During that time we did a massive cleanup of the clubroom and I received a puzzling phone call from a former middle school classmate that resulted in my going to watch a football game. When all was said and done, the new year was knocking on our door.

A new year, huh? I wonder what's going to happen. Personally, I need to do something about my grades or I'll be in serious trouble.

My mother wasn't being very subtle about her desire to send me to a cram school, so this would be the perfect opportunity to use my participation on a healthy sports team or in an official club of some sort as an excuse, but since I was a member of an unofficial and incomprehensible association that basically lounged around—at least, that was how it looked to other people—I could understand why someone would question the presence of a student with poor grades but planned on going to college.

For some reason Haruhi had ridiculously good grades, and based on the finals we just took Koizumi would also be considered smart. Asahina was also a diligent student, though it was possible that she was interested in studying ancient practices. And I shouldn't need to say anything about Nagato's grades.

"Well, I'll deal with it later."

First, I needed to make sure this winter trip was a success. That would be my only focus for now. I could do my studying in the next year. Since our mountain lodge countdown party had to start in this one.

And so, on that note—

"Off we go!"

Haruhi was yelling at the top of her lungs.

"Yahoo!"

Tsuruya was just as hyper.

"The weather at our destination is ideal for skiing at the moment."

Koizumi delivered an update on the forecast.

"So we're going skiing? As in the skiing where you glide on snow?"

Asahina lifted her chin, which was tightly secured by a scarf.

"..."

Nagato stood perfectly still with a small bag in one hand.

"Yay!"

My sister was jumping around.

We were in front of the station early this morning. We would be taking a train from here and switching to a connecting train before reaching the snowy mountain that was our destination at a little past noon. Which was fine, but why was my sister here when she wasn't supposed to be...?

"Who cares? Can't do anything about her tagging along. The easiest solution would be to bring her with us. She probably won't get in our way."

Haruhi hunched down and smiled at my sister.

"If it were somebody I didn't care about, I'd just chase them away, but your sister's a sweet girl, unlike you, so I'm perfectly fine with this. She also helped us out with the movie, and Shamisen will have someone to play with this way."

Yes, our family calico cat was a member of this trip. I shall refer you to the SOS Brigade's travel planner for an explanation.

"We will need a cat for the gimmick used in this particular mystery."

Something along the lines of The Cat Who..., I'm guessing.

Koizumi had taken a seat on his own luggage.

"A random cat would have sufficed, but Shamisen did an admirable job of acting when we were filming the movie. I was hoping for an encore performance."

The present Shamisen is just your typical domesticated cat that can't speak. You probably shouldn't expect much from him. I looked over at Haruhi, whose nose was practically touching my sister's.

"And as a result, she spotted me leaving."

Our departure was early in the morning and I had already told my mother to keep mum about the trip, so I wasn't very worried at the time. Since I figured that my sister didn't realize I was going on a trip with Haruhi and everybody else. But a surprising pitfall awaited me. I was in my room, stowing the slumbering Shamisen in a cat carrier, when my sister walked in for some inexplicable reason. She must have gone to the bathroom and, being half-asleep, stumbled into my room by mistake on her way back.

Things took off from there. My sister's eyes suddenly opened wide.

"Where are you taking Shami? Why are you dressed like that? Why are you packing?"

Wow, she's annoying. And after my eleven-year-old sister threw a fit that was exponentially worse than the one last summer, she latched onto my bag with both arms and legs like an oddly colored shellfish adhered to a rock.

"We can manage to accommodate another person," Koizumi said with a smile. "One additional child isn't going to put us over budget. I would agree with Suzumiya. There is no point in sending her home after she's come all the way out here."

My sister had finished jostling with Haruhi and proceeded to bury her face in Asahina's ample bosom and hug Nagato's perfectly still legs and shake, before she finally started squealing with laughter as Tsuruya swung her around.

Good thing I have a sister. If she were my brother, I'd have to take her to the back alley this very second.

*   *   *

My sister didn't slow down at all as she spent the duration of the express train ride to the snowy mountain jumping around us with glee and wasting energy. If she's too hyper now, she'll be tired out by the time we reach our destination, which means that I'll have to carry my sleeping sister once again, not that I would be able to accomplish anything by telling her this. Haruhi and Tsuruya were just as excited as she was and even the normally reserved Asahina seemed to be uncharacteristically enthusiastic about this trip. And Nagato of all people had given up on reading the paperback that she soon stuffed back into her bag, and she stared at my sister in silence.

I had my cheek against the window as I watched the scenery race by. Koizumi sat in the aisle seat next to me while Haruhi and the other girls sat in the seats before us. They turned the front row around so they would be facing one another and the five of them were now playing Uno. Don't make too much noise. You'll disturb the other passengers.

Koizumi and I were the odd ones out, left to play two-person old maid, but we soon gave up because it was too pointless. Why should a couple of guys have to entertain each other in this situation?

It would be more constructive to satiate my mental palate by fantasizing about how Asahina will look in ski gear. And then I proceeded to consider how I might manipulate the situation so the two of us could hit the ski slopes alone.

"Meow."

There was a sound coming from the pet carrier as a whisker poked through an opening.

After the movie mess was over with, Shamisen transformed into a cat that was so well-behaved you had to question if he actually was a former stray. He would sit and wait for us to bring him food, and he didn't pester us to play with him constantly. I would say that sleep was his top priority. He'd actually been asleep the whole time since I put him in this pet carrier, but the laziest of cats would still grow bored eventually. He was scratching at the door to signal that sentiment. Naturally I couldn't let him out while we were still on the train.

"Hang in there a little longer."

I directed those words toward the carrier at my feet.

"I'll give you something to munch on once we're there."

"Meow."

That was all it took for him to understand, apparently, as Shamisen once again fell quiet. Koizumi seemed to be impressed.

"I was considerably disturbed when he first started talking, but this cat was clearly the correct choice. And no, I don't mean that a male calico is particularly lucky. I'm referring to how he's an understanding and disciplined cat."

Haruhi was the one who randomly selected him from a swarm of stray cats. And since that managed to result in an extremely rare case, I was tempted to tell her to go buy a lottery ticket. It might help pay for SOS Brigade expenses. I was starting to have second thoughts about mooching off the literary club budget.

"A lottery ticket? Knowing Suzumiya, that would almost certainly complicate matters. Do you realize what could happen if she acquired a million dollars?"

I'd rather not think about it, but I can definitely see her buying a secondhand fighter jet from the American military. I could live with her possessing a single-seat aircraft, but if she managed to get her hands on a two-seater, well, it was pretty obvious who would get stuck in the back.

Or she might splurge on publicity. You'd be sitting back watching some prime-time show when the message THIS SHOW WAS BROUGHT

TO YOU BY THE SOS BRIGADE would pop up on the screen. I felt a shiver run down my spine when I pictured a commercial that featured us airing on national television right when families typically gathered around the TV. Nothing good could ever happen with Haruhi in a producer position. That was more apparent than the concept of a kindergartner's failing at the stock market.

"It is entirely possible that she would decide on a course of action that benefits humanity as a whole. Such as setting up a grant for inventions or funding research."

Koizumi offered what sounded to be a desperately optimistic point of view. Either way, it was never a good idea to gamble. After all, the stakes were too high here. High enough to make those risk-management people hesitate. Unless the reward made the risk worthwhile.

"Just have her buy one of those convenience store ice-cream bars that give you a chance for a second one free. That'll be enough."

I returned to enjoying the scenery as Koizumi leaned back in his seat and closed his eyes. We would probably be busy upon arrival at our destination, so it would be prudent to preserve my strength right now.

The landscape outside the window grew increasingly rural, and more snow appeared every time we passed through a tunnel. As I watched the scenery fly by, I eventually fell sound asleep.

And so the train ride ended and we gathered up our belongings and headed out of the station to find a two-colored sight, a clear blue sky and pristine white snow, along with a familiar-looking twosome who were greeting us in a ridiculously formal fashion.

"Welcome. We have been awaiting your arrival."

The most impressive butler I'd ever seen bowed deeply.

"You must be tired after the long trip. Please avail yourselves of our hospitality."

The suspiciously ageless and beautiful maid was also here.

"Hello, and thank you for your efforts."

Koizumi immediately walked up to stand next to them.

"I believe this would be the first meeting for Tsuruya. Here we have Arakawa and Mori, two acquaintances whom I asked to look after us for the duration of this trip."

They looked exactly the same as on that remote island last summer. The gray-haired Arakawa in a three-piece suit and Mori in a very plain apron dress that made it clear she was a maid.

"I am Arakawa."

"I am Mori."

They both bowed their heads at exactly the same time.

Did they refrain from wearing coats in this bitter cold as part of the performance, or were they so absorbed in their roles that a sense of professionalism kicked in?

Tsuruya was waving a heavy-looking bag around.

"Heya! Hi there. I shouldn't have anything to worry about if you come recommended by Koizumi. It's a pleasure to meet you. Feel free to use this lodge as you like!"

"Many thanks."

Arakawa took another courteous bow before lifting his face and revealing a dignified smile.

"I am pleased to see that everybody is doing well."

"My apologies for the inconvenience last summer."

Mori smiled gently as she spoke, and her smile grew softer when she saw my sister.

"My, what an adorable little guest."

The uninvited guest, my sister, returned to form faster than dried seaweed in boiling water as she gave a little cheer and leaped into Mori's skirt.

Haruhi had a wide smile on her face as she took a step onto the snow.

"Long time no see. I'm expecting this winter trip to be a blast. We were interrupted by that hurricane last summer so I wasn't able to fully enjoy myself, but I plan on compensating for that during this winter excursion."

Then she turned to us cheerfully, as though she had just queened a pawn.

"Now, everybody. We're going to go all out having fun here! Scrub away all the grime that's built up over the past year so we can be fresh to go when the new year comes around. You aren't allowed to bring any regrets into the next year. Got it?!"

We each responded in our own fashion. Tsuruya pumped her fist in the air as she attempted some semblance of a war cry, Asahina nodded nervously while tensing up, Koizumi was still smiling, Nagato didn't say a word, and my sister was still clinging to Mori.

And I was doing my best to avoid looking at Haruhi and her blindingly brilliant smile.

Nobody would expect a storm when there wasn't a single cloud in the beautiful blue sky.

At this point in time.

We piled into a couple of off-road trucks for the trek to the Tsuruya family vacation home. Arakawa and Mori were driving, which allowed me to deduce that Mori was at least old enough to obtain a driver's license. This information was actually helpful when you consider that I'd been wondering if she was our age. Not that any ulterior motives were involved here. We already had a hard-working maid in Asahina, so I didn't feel any particular attachment to Mori. That last part was especially important.

Our journey by automobile through the endless expanse of white didn't last very long. After fifteen minutes or so our big trucks came to a stop in front of a building that resembled a bed-and-breakfast type of lodge.

"The place certainly has atmosphere."

Haruhi was the first to hop out of the truck and onto the snow as she expressed her satisfaction.

"This particular vacation home is actually our smallest, though," Tsuruya remarked. "But I really love the place! It's a lot more comfortable this way."

Considering it was located near the train station, with a ski resort within walking distance, I would expect this place to be high-rent. Plus, Tsuruya probably wasn't joking when she said that it was the smallest of her family's vacation homes, given that she considered the sprawling Japanese mansion she called home to be the status quo. From a more pedestrian standpoint, this vacation home was just as big as the huge villa on the remote island we had visited the previous summer. How much evil had the Tsuruya family committed to be able to freely build such fancy houses all over the place?

"Welcome, everybody."

Arakawa the butler was showing us in. He and Mori had received from Tsuruya, along with the keys to the house, permission to come here one day before us, meaning that they had been preparing for our arrival since the previous day. This was largely thanks to Koizumi's being thorough in his planning and also thanks to Tsuruya's and her family's being so open-minded and generous.

As I gratefully entered the entirely wooden building that would certainly be fully booked every season if the Tsuruya family decided to transform their winter vacation home into a public lodge, I had a sudden premonition.

I didn't really understand what it was. Still, I could clearly feel that vague premonition pass through my mind.

"Hmm…?"

I looked around the interior of the vacation home and was impressed by what I saw.

Haruhi was all smiles as she lavished praise on Tsuruya, and

Tsuruya was laughing heartily in return. Koizumi was in a discussion with Arakawa and Mori. My sister had immediately taken Shamisen out of his pet carrier to hold in her arms, and Asahina was setting her belongings on the floor with a sigh of relief while Nagato merely stared at some indiscernible spot in the air.

Nothing seemed to be out of the ordinary.

We would spend the next few days on a spree of merrymaking disguised as a club foray before returning to our original location to enjoy everyday life…

Or so it should have gone.

The forthcoming murder would only be an act, not real. Haruhi was already aware of this fact, so we wouldn't need to worry about her going through emotional turmoil. Nagato and Asahina wouldn't have a role to play in this circus, and Koizumi would never have a chance to use his abnormal powers—

You could even say that this event was completely rigged. Nothing like a shady murder where nobody could guess what might happen. We wouldn't have to worry about anything out of the ordinary happening, like running into a cave cricket when checking on a person cooped up in his room.

Still, what was this feeling? This unsettling sensation that was like a ghost or some kind of apparition passing through my body. Yes, it reminded me of that odd, gnawing sensation I experienced when I hadn't yet realized that the second half of summer was in an endless loop. But I wouldn't consider this to be déjà vu…

"No use."

The sensation evaded my reach the way a slimy fish would slip out of my grasp.

"Must be my imagination."

I shook my head and picked up my stuff as I began to ascend the staircase and make my way to the room I had been assigned. The interior wasn't particularly fancy, but I wasn't exactly an expert at appraisal. I'm guessing that if I asked how much this simple-looking banister cost to install, I would almost certainly be informed of a material and personnel cost that would make my jaw drop.

I soon reached the second-floor hallway where the bedrooms were.

"Say, Kyon."

Tsuruya walked over with a smile on her face.

"Mind sharing a room with your sister? Truth be told, there were barely enough rooms for everybody. The attic room I used when I was a child is open, but she'd probably feel lonely if we stuck her up there, yeah?"

"I don't mind sharing a room with her."

Haruhi came butting in.

"I just checked our rooms and the beds are huge. You could fit three people side by side with plenty of room to spare. And it would be safer with two girls sharing a room instead, right?"

I don't see why you think that it would be dangerous for me to share a room with my sister. Sharing a room with Asahina would probably test my mental and spiritual fortitude, but sharing a room with my sister would be the same as sharing a room with Shamisen, as far as I was concerned.

"Well, how about it?"

Haruhi's question was directed at my sister, who had Shamisen clinging to one shoulder. My sister giggled and blurted out an answer that completely disregarded our previous exchange.

"I wanna sleep in Mikuru's room."

And so my sister was able to slip into Asahina's room, which left me to take care of Shamisen in my room. I might as well dump this cat on someone while I'm at it.

"I will have to refuse. Unlike yours, my nerves aren't strong enough to bear the strain of spending time with a talking cat."

Koizumi refused my generous offer, which led to Nagato staring at the calico for thirty seconds or so.

"No."

And with that curt response she turned her back on me.

Well, I could probably just let him wander around the building. Shamisen didn't seem to pay any heed to the fact that he was in a strange house as he jumped onto my bed the way he did at home and promptly dozed off, despite having slept for most of the train ride. I was tempted to lie down next to him, but our schedule didn't allow for any breaks, as we had been ordered by Haruhi to assemble downstairs before we even had a chance to settle in.

"Now, let's go! Skiing!"

I had a feeling that she was moving a little too fast, but we apparently didn't have a second to waste if we were to light up the place as Haruhi demanded. And the addition of Tsuruya, a regular bundle of energy who could possibly top Haruhi when it came to hyperactivity, only served to double the effect.

Koizumi had rented the skiwear and skis somewhere. I found it odd how he'd managed to take our measurements without our knowing about it. There was even a full set for my sister, who had joined in at the last second, that was a perfect fit. I could picture agents from the "Agency" (black suits and black sunglasses) sneaking into North High and my sister's grade school and shuffling through student medical records in the nurse's office. Hmm, I should ask them for Asahina's measurements later. Not that I would be able to do anything with them, but still, I was curious.

"It's been forever since I skied," Haruhi said. "The last time was during an event for kids when I was in grade school. It never snows where we live. Can't have winter without snow."

A view that could only come from someone who lived in an area without regular snow. I'm willing to bet that there are plenty of people out there who could live without seeing another snowflake ever again. I would even draw the conclusion that Kenshin Uesugi from the Warring States period would fall into that category.

We marched along in our clumsy boots, carrying our skis, before finally reaching a rather impressive-looking ski slope. Like Haruhi, I hadn't skied in a long time. Not since middle school, I think. Pretty sure that this was my sister's first time and it was apparently Asahina's as well. I was almost positive that Nagato had never skied before, but I was pretty confident that she would be skiing like a pro the second we hit the slopes.

As we rode the lift, I could see skiwear flashing in every color. I was wondering why there weren't very many people around when Tsuruya elaborated on the reason.

"This place isn't that famous. Just a quiet place to ski for the people who know about it. After all, this was our private ski resort until ten years ago."

But it was open to the public now, according to Tsuruya's explanation, which was completely free of scorn. I guess that there are actually people in this world with charisma, character, money, and pedigree. People so perfect that you can't do a thing about them.

Once we got off the lift, Haruhi put her skis on and turned to me.

"What are you going to do, Kyon? I'd prefer to head on over to the expert course, but I'm not sure if everybody knows how to ski. Do you?"

"Give us some time to practice."

I managed to successfully attach the skis to my boots, but my sister and Asahina were tripping over themselves every twelve inches as we watched.

"We need to teach them the basics or else they'll have trouble getting back on a ski lift, let alone attacking the expert course."

Asahina, already covered in snow, looked as though she had

been born to be dressed in skiwear. Sometimes I find myself wondering if there is a single article of clothing in this world that wouldn't look good on her.

"In that case I'll coach Mikuru through the motions while Harls, you take charge of the little sister! Kyon and everybody else can just ski around!"

Couldn't ask for a better plan. It would take me a while to get the hang of skiing again. I glanced to my side real quick.

"…"

Nagato, stone-faced and with a firm grip on her poles, had already zoomed off without a hitch.

In the end my sister failed to learn anything. Wasn't there something wrong with how Haruhi was teaching her?

"Line up your legs and push off hard with the poles like *oomph* and then off you go *zoom* and *whoosh* to accelerate and once you need to stop, just go *roar*. That should do the trick."

It didn't. If life were so simple, we would have developed cars that were perfectly environmentally friendly by now. Unfortunately, my sister was only able to extend the distance between tumbles from about a foot to a yard. Still, she seemed to be enjoying herself as she tumbled around all over the place and gleefully gobbled down snow, so I guess it really didn't matter if she didn't learn how to ski as long as she managed to entertain herself. And stop eating that stuff or you'll end up with a stomachache.

Meanwhile, either Asahina had natural talent for skiing or Tsuruya was a brilliant instructor, since Asahina was able to master the art after thirty minutes.

"Whoa, whoa! This is fun. Wow, it's amazing."

A description of Asahina as she skied with a smile on her face against the white backdrop would probably drag, so I'll try to summarize. It was like watching the descendant of a stylish snow woman suddenly appear in the modern world. An artistic masterpiece that was satisfying enough for me to make a U-turn and head home this very second. I would need to take a picture first, though.

Haruhi continued to direct sideways glances at Koizumi and me as we trained on our own, while she stared pensively at my sister, who was failing to make any progress at all. The look on her face clearly said that she was in a hurry to run up to the top of the mountain and race down, but she couldn't take this fifth grader along for the ride.

Tsuruya must have been thinking the same thing.

"Harls, you guys can go ahead and ride the lift to the top!"

Tsuruya was helping up my sister, who was cheerfully waving her arms around after falling on her face again.

"I'll take responsibility for looking after this girl! We can make a snowman if she likes! Sledding would also work! We can probably borrow one somewhere!"

"Are you sure?"

Haruhi watched as Tsuruya and my sister jostled with each other.

"Thanks. Sorry about this."

"It's no biggie! Well, little sister! Do you want a skiing lesson, a snowman session, or a sled ride?"

"Snowman!"

My sister gave her answer in a loud voice as Tsuruya laughed and began to remove her skis.

"Okay, snowman it is. We're going to make a huge one. A huge one!"

The two of them immediately began to make a snowman while Asahina watched enviously.

"A snowman, huh? Ah, I might want to join them…"

"No."

Haruhi swiftly placed a firm lock on Asahina's arm before smiling at her.

"Our destination is the peak. We can all race. The first person to reach the foot of the slope will be granted the title General Winter. Let's all try our best."

I had a feeling that she wouldn't let us stop until she won. That I could live with, but the idea of heading straight for the peak of the slope was a little scary. We should take this step by step.

Haruhi just snorted.

"Pathetic. It's more fun to face these challenges head-on."

And yet she actually decided to go with my idea, for once. First we would try the intermediate course, and save the main event, the expert course, for the very end.

"Let's get on the lift. Yuki! We're going now! Come back!"

Nagato had been gliding in wide arcs around us, but as soon as she heard Haruhi's voice she turned back and made a perfect stop right next to me, shaving off a layer of snow in the process.

"We'll be racing one another, okay? I got enough free lift passes for everybody, so we can go until the sun sets…no! We can keep going after the sun sets. Come now, everybody follow me."

Don't need you ordering us through every single action we take. And if I were to request permission to join the snowman team, I would probably be denied. Koizumi aside, if I left Nagato and Asahina alone with Haruhi when she went on a rampage, we'd instantly go from blizzard to ice age. There needed to be an objective supervisor around at all times. Not that I would claim to be a particularly objective person. Well, I wasn't entirely sure what I was saying, and Koizumi would probably have an easy time picking apart my reasoning, so I gave up on that line of thought. After all, I stopped caring about that crap a long time ago.

All the members were safely here in one piece, the snow was nice and powdery so there weren't any complaints in that department,

and the sky was clear and blue as far as the eye could see. Our brigade chief extended one arm with a smile that was as sunny as said sky.

"These lifts only seat two each. To be fair, we'll use rock, paper, scissors to decide."

Now then.

Nothing significant happened after that point. Leaving Tsuruya and my sister behind, the official SOS Brigade members took the lift up the slopes and enjoyed the experience of skiing without incident. The snowman was closer to completion every time we reached the bottom of the slope, and Tsuruya and my sister were joking around with each other like they were the same age while they placed a bucket on the snowman's head and added eyes and a nose. They were certainly enjoying themselves. In fact, they even started working on a second snowman, which would be my most recent memory of them.

And perhaps, my last memory of them.

I'm not sure how many times we raced down that slope.

After safely making our way to the bottom, we discovered that out of nowhere…I mean, we literally had no idea where it came from, but all of a sudden, we were in the middle of a blizzard. Whiteout conditions. Couldn't see anything beyond a yard or so.

The howling winds sent the snow pounding against our bodies. The pain from that relentless barrage was actually worse than the bitter cold. I could feel my exposed face begin to freeze and I was forced to keep my face down when I tried to breathe. This was one crazy blizzard.

And it came without any warning.

Haruhi had been in the lead when she came to a stop and Nagato, close behind, also came to a sudden halt. By the time Asahina and I, who were skiing along at a leisurely pace, and Koizumi, bringing up the rear, caught up to them—

The blizzard was already here.

As if it had been summoned by someone.

...

......

....

That concludes my flashback. I hope that you now understand why we're trudging around this snowy mountain.

After all, we couldn't see a thing out here. There might be a cliff a few yards ahead that we could walk straight off without knowing. There shouldn't be any cliffs around here, but I wouldn't be surprised to see one pop up in a place where nothing was on the map. I had no intention of trying large-hill ski jumping without a ramp. I guess that my example of cliffs was a little exaggerated, but there was a realistic chance of one of us crashing into a snow-covered tree that was impossible to see and breaking a nose or something.

"Where are we right now?"

Times like this are when we can depend on Nagato. I was reluctant to rely on her, but our lives were on the line here. Yet we were still lost after hours of following Nagato's exact navigation, as I mentioned in the beginning.

"That's odd."

Haruhi's muttering was beginning to carry a tone of suspicion.

"What's going on here? It makes no sense that we haven't seen a single person yet. How long have we been walking around?"

Her gaze was directed at Nagato, who led the way. She was questioning if Nagato had gone the wrong way. The only logical conclusion that could be drawn in this situation. We were walking through a ski resort, not some unexplored wilderness. If we continued to walk in a direction that took us down the slope, we would inevitably reach the bottom, or else something was clearly wrong.

"I guess we don't really have a choice, so let's build an igloo and take shelter. Until the blizzard dies down."

"Wait."

I stopped Haruhi as I struggled through the whipping snow to reach Nagato's side.

"What's going on?"

The girl with no expression on her face slowly looked up at me, her short hair frozen stiff.

"An indeterminate phenomenon."

Her voice was soft. Her black eyes were staring at me earnestly.

"If the spatial coordinates I have identified for our position are correct, we have already passed the starting point."

What the hell? Wouldn't that mean that we should have spotted some sign of civilization by now? I mean, we haven't even spotted any lift cables or a lodge of any kind.

"The situation has transcended my capacity for spatial perception."

I sucked in a deep breath when I heard Nagato's calm voice. I could feel crystals of snow evaporate as they touched the tip of my tongue, along with any words I could have said.

A situation that's beyond Nagato's abilities?

Was this what that vague premonition had been hinting at?

"Who's responsible this time?"

"..."

Nagato fell silent, as if deep in thought, while she stared at the frenzied dance of snowflakes without batting an eye.

None of us had brought a watch or cell phone when we hit the slopes, so we didn't even know the current time. I think that we left the Tsuruya family vacation home around 3 PM. And it'd been a few hours since then. The cloudy sky was still illuminated by a faint glimmer of light. Still, the thick clouds and howling blizzard prevented us from determining how high the sun was in the sky. After all, the lighting was about as dim as that of a cave with luminous moss, and a strange rusty taste seeped out from my wisdom teeth, followed by a slight pain.

A wall of snow blocked us in every direction and we were blanketed by a canopy of gray.

This scene seemed a little too similar to another experience.

Don't tell me that—

"Ah!"

Haruhi yelled at the top of her lungs right next to my ears, which scared me so much that my heart almost shattered my rib cage and jumped out of my chest.

"Hey, don't scare me like that. Stop screaming in my ear."

"Kyon, look over there."

Haruhi pointed, her finger standing firm against the wind—

And there was a faint light in the distance.

"What?"

I squinted. The blustering snow made it seem like the light was flickering, but that wasn't the case. The glow was about as dim as a firefly's after mating.

"It's coming from a window."

Haruhi's voice was filled with excitement.

"There's a building over there. We can ask them for shelter. Or else we're going to freeze to death at this rate."

Her prediction would soon become reality if we didn't do something. But a building? Out here in the middle of nowhere?

"This way! Mikuru, Koizumi. Follow my lead."

Haruhi was like a human plow as she clawed open a path before us. The cold, anxiety, and fatigue must have gotten to Asahina, as her body was visibly shaking while Koizumi shielded her and the two of them trailed after Haruhi. As Koizumi passed me, he whispered something to me that sent a chill through my heart.

"The light is clearly artificial. However, it wasn't there a moment ago. I am sure of this, as I have been paying close attention to our surroundings."

"…"

Nagato and I remained silent as we watched Haruhi use her skis to kick away snow and open a path.

"Hurry, hurry! Kyon, Yuki! Don't fall behind!"

There was no other option. I would rather gamble on a slim chance for survival than freeze to death and show up in the news a hundred years later. It didn't matter if this was a trap, since we really didn't have a choice at this point.

I steered Nagato before me as we set off on the path through the snow that Haruhi had made.

As we approached the light, its identity became clear. I was forced to grudgingly admit that Haruhi's superhuman vision was worthy of praise. The light was plainly coming from the window of a building.

"It's a mansion. And a huge one to boot…"

Haruhi paused for a moment as she looked straight up at the structure and gave us her impression before she set off again.

I also looked up at the towering building as my mood darkened. The mansion stood against the white snow and gray sky like a silhouette. I wasn't about to solely attribute the ominous aura I felt to its outward appearance. And the building was more castle than mansion, considering the spires (whose purpose was unknown) that protruded from the roof, and the inadequate lighting, or what would be considered dark décor in general. And this structure was in the middle of some snowy mountains. If this wasn't suspect, you would have to round up every dictionary in the country and rewrite the definition of that word.

A blizzard on a snowy mountain. Where we were stranded. When we happened to spot a faint light as we had completely lost our sense of direction. And then we arrived at an odd-looking mansion of Western make—

With so many conditions met, the next step would be the arrival of the suspicious-looking owner of this mansion, or perhaps some kind of grotesque monster? So, is this story going to be mystery or horror?

"Excuse me!"

Haruhi was already yelling at the entrance. There wasn't an intercom or door knocker to speak of. Haruhi was beating on the rustic door with her fist.

"Is anybody home?!"

I looked up at the mansion again from my position behind Haruhi as she pounded away.

In any case, this situation, setting, and stage felt a little too convenient for my tastes. I could tell that this wasn't Koizumi's doing. Though it would certainly be great if the door were to open and reveal Arakawa and Mori bowing deeply... But that obviously wasn't going to happen after Nagato had attested that the circumstances were beyond her own capabilities. I doubt that Koizumi could ever upstage Nagato, and even if Nagato happened to be in on the prank, she would never lie to me.

Haruhi continued to shriek in an ear-piercing voice that held its own against the howling blizzard.

"We're lost! Could you let us rest for a bit?! We're going to die if we have to keep standing out here in the snow!"

I looked back to make sure that everybody was here. Nagato was staring at Haruhi's back, doing her typical bisque-doll impression. Asahina was hugging herself with a terrified look on her face.

Koizumi had dropped his usual smile as he stood with his arms crossed, his head cocked, and an expression on his face like he had just eaten something bitter. He was about as indecisive as Hamlet as he visibly wondered if we should open the door or not.

Haruhi was starting to make enough noise to be considered guilty of disturbing the peace, at least in my neighborhood. Despite that, there had been no response from the inside.

"Nobody's home?"

Haruhi removed her gloves and breathed warm air onto her hands with a bitter expression on her face.

"I thought there'd be somebody around, since the lights are on…What do we do, Kyon?"

It'd be rather difficult for me to give you an immediate answer to that question. The job of rushing headlong into an obvious trap belonged to your typical emotional and hotheaded superhero.

"We just need a place to shelter us from the snow and wind…Is there a shed or something nearby?"

However, Haruhi disregarded my suggestion to search the vicinity. I watched as she put her gloves back on and grabbed the doorknob that was covered by snow and ice. From the side, it almost looked like she was praying as she exhaled. And with a serious look on her face, Haruhi slowly turned the doorknob.

I probably should have stopped her. Or at the very least I should have asked for Nagato's advice before making a decision. But it was too late now—

It almost felt like the mansion was opening its gaping maw.

As the door opened.

Artificial light fell across our faces.

"It wasn't locked. You'd think that somebody would answer the door if they're home."

Haruhi set her skis and poles against the wall before stomping in ahead of the rest of us.

"Hello?! Anybody home?! We're coming in!"

Beggars can't be choosers. We followed our brigade chief's lead. Koizumi was the last one in as he shut the door, and we were finally able to bid a temporary farewell to the biting cold and deafening wind that had plagued us for the past few hours. A momentary sigh of relief.

"Whew…"

Asahina plunked herself down on the floor.

"Hey, nobody around?!"

As I listened to Haruhi's ear-piercing voice, I could feel the light and warmth seep into my bones. The same feeling you would get when sinking into a warm bath after standing outside in the middle of winter. The snow on my head and skiwear was melting and dripping water onto the floor. The heat was definitely on.

But there was no sign of human life. By now some aggravated person should have come storming in to kick Haruhi out, but nobody was responding.

"This better not be a haunted house."

I muttered to myself as I looked around the interior of the mansion. The entrance led directly into a large room. The best comparison I can make is to the lobby of a fancy hotel. The atrium-shaped ceiling was awfully high up there, with an awfully massive chandelier that provided flickering light. The floor was covered by a carpet of deep crimson. The structure may have appeared to be some kind of bizarre castle from the outside, but the interior was pretty modern. The middle of the room was occupied by an extensive staircase that connected to the second floor. All we needed was a checkroom to complete this phony hotel experience.

"I'm going to take a look around."

Haruhi was already sick of waiting for the mansion owner, who had yet to appear. She squirmed out of her soggy skiwear in a way that could only be described as "molting" and kicked off her ski boots.

"I doubt that anyone will blame us for coming in without permission, since this is an emergency, but I wouldn't want them to make a fuss about it later. I'll go see if anybody's here. You guys can wait here."

That was the brigade chief we know and love. Haruhi was behaving exactly the way a leader should as she took off running in her socks.

"Wait."

I was the one who stopped her.

"I'm coming with you. If I let you go by yourself, I won't be able to stop worrying about the chance of you doing something rude or insulting."

I removed my skiwear and boots in a rush, and my body instantly felt lighter as I seemingly shed the fatigue from walking around the mountains in the middle of a blizzard along with those outer garments. I handed the bulky clothing to the person who was conveniently standing nearby.

"Koizumi, I'm trusting you to take care of Asahina and Nagato."

The esper freak who had failed to be of any use in getting off this snowy mountain shot me a crooked smile and nodded. I took one last glance at Asahina, who was looking up at me with worried eyes, and Nagato, who stood perfectly still in silence.

"Let's go. The place is so big that it's possible they couldn't hear you in the back."

"Don't order me around. In these situations, you only need one person in a leadership role! Now do as I say."

Haruhi's competitive nature was on full display here as she grabbed my wrist and turned to the three brigade members on standby.

"We'll be right back. Koizumi, you need to look after the other two."

"Roger that."

Koizumi was back to his usual smile as he replied to Haruhi and gave me a slight nod.

I'm pretty sure that he was thinking the same thing I was.

We could search every nook and cranny of this mansion without finding a single person.

I just had a hunch somehow.

Haruhi chose to search the next floor first. Once we ascended the large staircase by the entrance, we arrived at a long hallway that stretched into the distance to right and left and was littered with more wooden doors than I could count. I tried opening one of the doors, and it swung open readily to reveal a Western-style bedroom.

There were more stairs at both ends of the hallway, and Haruhi and I headed up another flight. I let Haruhi lead the way.

"That way. Now this way."

Haruhi used one hand to point the direction while using her other hand to pull me along by my wrist. I had the urge to cover my ears every time we reached a new floor and Haruhi yelled out, "Anybody home?!" but I wasn't allowed to do that either. All I could do was follow her orders and tag along.

There were so many doors that we could only manage to open a few at random. As we confirmed that they all led to similar-looking bedrooms, we arrived at the fourth floor. I wasn't sure if the hallways of the mansion were supposed to be lit at night, but every floor was brightly illuminated.

I was in the process of eyeballing the doors and deciding which to open next when Haruhi broke the silence.

"This reminds me of last summer. When we went outside to check on the boat."

…Right, something like this happened back then. I vaguely recalled Haruhi dragging me through a downpour the same way she was dragging me around right now.

As I rewound the sepia-colored film that composed my memory, Haruhi came to an abrupt halt and so did I, as she was still clutching my wrist.

"You know."

Haruhi began to speak in a subdued tone.

"I forget when this started, but it kind of just happened…I decided to take a different path from most people. Ah, I don't mean a literal path that you walk on. I'm talking about a path in the sense of what direction I want to go. As in a career path or way of life."

"Uh-huh," I responded in a noncommittal tone. What's your point?

"My point is that I have been purposely avoiding any path that the general public would follow. I mean, it wouldn't be any fun to go with the flow and do what everybody else does. I don't get why anyone would voluntarily choose to lead a boring life. That was when I realized. If I went against the norm from the very beginning, I might end up having a lot more fun."

Your typical rebellious spirit would blindly shun anything mainstream and support the obscure, regardless of the benefit or lack thereof. Personally, I more or less felt inclined to subscribe to that particular creed, so I could see where Haruhi was coming from. Still, I have a feeling that you take things to such extremes that concepts like "mainstream" no longer apply.

Haruhi chuckled in a creepy tone.

"Well, none of that really matters."

What? Don't ask me for my opinion if you aren't going to listen. Do you understand the predicament we're in? We don't have time to joke around and take it easy.

"Anyway, there's something that's been bugging me."

"What is it now?"

My reply carried a tinge of irritation.

"Did something happen between you and Yuki?"

…

Haruhi wasn't looking at me. She stared down the hallway before us.

I waited a beat before responding.

"…What are you talking about? Nothing happened."

"Liar. You've been paying extra attention to Yuki since Christmas Eve. Every time I check, you're looking Yuki's way."

Haruhi was still looking down the hallway.

"It's not because you hit your head, is it? Or what? You better not have any funny ideas involving Yuki."

I wasn't aware of the fact that I had been constantly staring at Nagato. At most, I'd been staring at her sixty percent of the time, with Asahina occupying the other forty percent…except this wasn't the time to be saying that.

"Well…"

I could only manage to stammer a feeble reply. As Haruhi had noticed, I'd been trying to be more considerate of Nagato since the disappearance mess, so I felt uncomfortable about denying my concern flat out. Still, I never expected Haruhi to notice, so I didn't have an appropriate answer ready for her, but I couldn't tell her the truth either.

"Spit it out."

Haruhi was being deliberate in enunciating her words.

"Yuki's been acting weird too. She doesn't look different, but I can tell. You must have done something to Yuki."

She'd gone from warning me about having any funny ideas to accusing me of already doing something in the space of two to three sentences. It was entirely possible that if I left her alone, she would reach the conclusion that something had actually happened between Nagato and me by the time we made it back to where Koizumi and the girls were waiting. Though something actually had happened, which made it difficult for me to simply deny her allegation outright.

"Ah. You see…"

"I won't let you smooth-talk your way out of this. Disgusting."

"You've got it wrong. Neither of us has done anything to be ashamed of. Uh…The truth is…"

Haruhi was looking at me like I was an archery target.

"The truth is?"

As Haruhi stared me down, I finally came up with something to say.

"Nagato has this problem she's dealing with. Yeah, that's it. She asked me for advice a while back."

It's pretty hard to think and talk at the same time. Especially when you're making up an entire story.

"Truth be told, her problem hasn't been solved yet. I guess that…basically…it's something Nagato needs to deal with herself. I can only listen and try to help her figure out what she wants to do. Nagato doesn't have a solution yet, so I'm still a little concerned. Which is probably why I keep looking in her direction."

"What kind of problem? And why would she ask you for help? She could have come to me instead."

Haruhi still sounded suspicious.

"I doubt that Yuki would rely on you more than Koizumi or me."

"She probably would have taken anyone that wasn't you."

Haruhi's eyebrows narrowed, but I used my free hand to stop her. My mind was finally becoming clear.

"Here's a basic rundown. Do you know why Nagato's living alone?"

"Family issues, right? I don't know any details, since I find it disgusting to pry into someone else's private matters."

"There's been some change in her family situation. Depending on how everything turns out, Nagato might not be living alone anymore."

"What do you mean?"

"Simply put, she'll be moving. Out of that apartment to a faraway place...to live with relatives perhaps. Naturally, she'll have to switch schools. Transfer out, if you will. They might time it so she's in a different high school next spring when we all become second-years..."

"Really?"

Haruhi's expression softened. I've got this.

"Yeah, but Nagato doesn't want to transfer schools, regardless of how it goes with her family. She wants to stay at North High until graduation."

"So that's been on her mind..."

Haruhi lowered her head for a moment before looking back up at me, an expression of rage on her face.

"All the more reason to come to me, then. Yuki is an important brigade member. I'm not going to let her run off without a word."

Those words were all I needed to hear.

"If she had gone to you, you would have made everything more complicated. Knowing you, you'd probably march off to the home of Nagato's relatives and start a protest against her transferring."

"Probably."

"Nagato is determined to settle this herself. She's a little unsure at the moment, but her heart lies in the clubroom. It's just that she's been brooding over this by herself for so long that it's been an emotional strain on her. She probably wanted to talk to somebody else about it. This was when I was in the hospital, so Nagato told me everything when she came to visit by herself. I just happened to be there at the time when nobody else was. That's all it was."

"I see..."

Haruhi sighed softly.

"Yuki, huh…I didn't realize she was having problems. Looked like she was having fun to me. Before winter vacation started, I was walking through the hallway when I ran into some of the computer society underlings saluting her. And she didn't seem to mind…"

I tried to picture Nagato with a pleased look on her face, but I couldn't so I just shook my head to clear my thoughts. Haruhi suddenly lifted her face.

"But, mmm, well, yeah. I guess that sounds like the Yuki I know."

I was able to breathe a sigh of relief as she apparently bought my story. I found it odd that she could attribute any part of this made-up scenario to typical Nagato behavior, but it seemed that my tale-spinning matched Haruhi's impression of Nagato. I tried to wrap things up.

"Everything I just said is off the record. You definitely can't tell Nagato. Don't worry. She'll still be reading quietly in the clubroom when the new school year starts."

"Of course. I wouldn't have it any other way."

"But."

The wrist caught in Haruhi's iron grip was starting to feel very warm as I continued.

"If, on the off chance that Nagato ends up deciding to transfer schools or is taken away against her will, you're free to go on a rampage. If it comes to that, I'll back you every step of the way."

Haruhi blinked a couple of times before staring up at me in a daze. And then she flashed me an absolutely dazzling smile.

"Of course!"

Haruhi and I made our way back to the entrance lobby on the first floor, where we were treated to three idiosyncratic greetings by the members, who had removed their skiwear while waiting for us.

For some reason, Asahina was on the verge of tears.

"Kyon, Suzumiya…I'm so glad that you're back…"

"Mikuru, why are you crying? I said that we'd be right back."

Haruhi patted Asahina's hair in good humor, but the expression on Koizumi's face ruined the moment. What's with the eye contact? You're not going to grab my heart with looks that don't make any sense at all.

The last member, Nagato, just stood there in a haze and stared at Haruhi with her black eyes. She seemed to be even more out of it than usual, but I just assumed that an alien-made organic lifeform would be hard-pressed to carry out the task of plowing a path through the snow like one of those Russell snowplows. This assumption also took into account the fact that Nagato wasn't perfect. I was fully aware of that now.

"Do you have a moment?"

Koizumi casually walked over to me and whispered in my ear.

"I would like to keep this a secret from Suzumiya."

When you put it that way, I don't have any choice but to listen.

"A rough estimate will do. How much time would you say has passed since you and Suzumiya left us?"

"Hasn't even been half an hour."

During that time, I had to listen to Haruhi's little speech and make up a story to tell her, but it didn't feel that long to me.

"I was expecting you to say that."

I couldn't tell if Koizumi was satisfied or disturbed by my response.

"For those of us who were left behind, three hours have passed since you and Suzumiya set off on your search."

Nagato was the one who kept track of time, according to Koizumi.

"Since you were taking so long to return."

He brushed aside his bangs, now dry, before flashing me a nihilistic smile.

"So I came up with a little experiment. I requested Nagato to move to a slightly removed location that was out of sight. We synchronized our count first, and then I asked her to return after ten minutes."

Nagato apparently complied without complaint. She walked down a hallway to the side of the entrance before eventually turning the corner and vanishing from sight—

"However, Nagato returned before I could count to two hundred. I found this puzzling, as less than three minutes had passed in my mind. However, Nagato asserted that she had positively counted to ten minutes."

Nagato was obviously correct. You must have nodded off or counted wrong.

"Asahina was also counting in a soft voice and our counts were very close."

Well then…I still think that Nagato would be the one who's right, though.

"I have no intention of questioning the accuracy of Nagato's count. It shouldn't be possible for her to make simple arithmetic mistakes."

So we're in the realm of what else could it be?

"The flow of time varies within this mansion depending on your location…or your sense of time becomes distorted here. Either explanation is valid. It's possible that both apply."

Koizumi glanced over at Haruhi, who was in the process of roughing up Asahina before turning back to me.

"It would be best to move together as a group. Or else our sense of time will become increasingly distorted. That is not all. If the temporal deviation is limited to the interior of this building, we can still cope. However, what if the distortion began before we were seemingly lured into this place? How did you feel about the sudden blizzard and our inability to reach the bottom of the slope?

If we were to assume that we had already slipped into a different dimension at that point..."

I looked at Asahina, whose hair had been disheveled by Haruhi, before turning to Nagato. Her hair, which had been turned into a mess by the blizzard, was now dry and restored to its original state. Her skin was a warmer white than the snow.

I whispered my reply to Koizumi.

"Knowing you, you probably already discussed this with Nagato and Asahina. Did they say anything?"

"Asahina didn't even know where to begin."

I can see that. I was referring more to the other girl.

Koizumi lowered his voice another notch.

"She didn't respond. When I asked her to participate in my experiment, she walked off without saying a word. And she was silent after she returned. When I asked if ten minutes had actually passed, she just nodded. She didn't express herself in any other way."

Nagato was staring at the red carpet. Her lack of expression was nothing new, but was it just my imagination or was she spacing out more than usual?

I moved to express my concern to Nagato.

"Kyon, what are you doing? We need to report to everyone."

Haruhi interrupted me with a glare before continuing in a voice that made it sound like she was bragging about a big catch.

"We went through the whole place and every room from the second floor up was a bedroom. I was hoping to find a telephone somewhere..."

"Yeah, there weren't any," I chimed in. "And there weren't any TVs or radios. No phone jacks or wireless devices either."

"I see."

Koizumi stroked his chin with his fingertips.

"In other words, we have no means of communicating with or receiving information from the outside world."

"Not in any room that's on the second floor or up."

Haruhi's smile didn't show the slightest hint of anxiety.

"I hope there's something on the first floor. There should be, right? Considering how big this mansion is, there's probably a special room just for communication purposes. So let's go find it!" Haruhi exclaimed as she pumped one fist in the air like a banner and dragged the gloomy Asahina with her.

Koizumi and I followed her lead, with Nagato trailing a few steps behind.

We soon reached the dining hall. An area furnished with antique decorations that was as fancy, spacious, and flashy as what you'd find in a three-star restaurant, not that I've ever been in one. The dining table was covered by a white tablecloth and golden candelabras. I looked up at the ceiling to find a fancy chandelier coldly looking down at the SOS Brigade members.

"There really isn't anybody around."

Haruhi spoke as she lifted a steaming teacup to her mouth.

"I wonder what happened to the people here. The lights and heating were all left on. What a waste of electricity. And there isn't a communications room or anything. What's going on here?"

The hot milk tea Haruhi was currently sipping had been borrowed without permission from the kitchen at the back of this restaurant-like dining hall, along with cups and a kettle. While Asahina was waiting for the water to boil, she and Haruhi had checked the various cabinets to find neatly stacked tableware that was sparkling clean as though it had just been washed and dried. The extremely large refrigerator was stocked with plenty of food. All things considered, I found it difficult to believe that the mansion had been abandoned for an extended period. It was almost like the inhabitants of the mansion had all packed up and left the second before we arrived. No, that explanation was also questionable. If that were the case, there would still be traces of human life.

"It's like the *Mary Celeste*."

Haruhi probably meant that as a joke, but I wasn't laughing.

The five of us had searched the first floor together. We walked single file through the hallways, checking every door we came across to scrounge around for useful items. We also discovered a laundry room with a giant dryer, a karaoke room with brand-new machines, a bath that was as big as the ones you would find in public bathhouses, and a recreation room equipped with a pool table, Ping-Pong table, and automated mah-jongg table...

I could only hope that these rooms hadn't popped out of nowhere in the past twenty-four hours.

"There is another possible explanation."

Koizumi set his cup on the saucer and picked up one of the shining candelabras as if he were playing with it. For a moment I almost thought that he was going to swipe it, but he soon placed it back on the table after a thorough appraisal.

"The inhabitants of this mansion went on a long trip before the blizzard hit and the bad weather is inhibiting their return."

He smiled thinly at Haruhi.

"In that case, they will return once the blizzard dies down. Hopefully, they will forgive us for coming in without permission."

"I'm sure they will. We didn't have a choice. Ah, maybe this mansion is set up to be an emergency shelter for skiers who get lost? That would explain why it's empty."

"I don't think you can have an emergency shelter without a phone or radio."

My voice was fatigued. That was the only thing I had learned after the five of us walked around the entire first floor. Not only had we failed to find any means of communication or source of outside news, there wasn't a single clock in the building.

Even worse, I was starting to get the feeling that this mansion ignored a lot of building and fire codes.

"Who would build such a large and inconvenient emergency shelter?"

"The federal or municipal government? It's probably funded by tax money. In that case, I don't need to feel bad about drinking this tea. I pay taxes so I have a right to use these facilities. ...Right, I'm feeling hungry so let's make something. Give me a hand, Mikuru."

Once Haruhi made up her mind, she ignored everybody else. She swiftly took Asahina's hand.

"Huh? Ah, y-yes!"

Asahina gave us a worried look as she was dragged to the kitchen. I felt bad for her, but I was concerned about the flow-of-time issue Koizumi was talking about, so I needed Haruhi to make herself scarce.

"Nagato."

I turned to the girl with short hair, who was staring at her empty ceramic cup.

"What's up with this mansion? Where are we?"

Nagato remained frozen in position. After thirty seconds or so, she finally opened her mouth.

"This space is putting strain on me."

That remark came out of nowhere.

I don't get it. What does she mean? Can't Nagato contact her creator or patron or whatever and get them to deal with this? This is an abnormal situation. Shouldn't they lend us a hand every now and then?

Nagato finally turned to look my way, but there was no expression on her face.

"My link to the Data Overmind has been cut off. Cause cannot be determined."

Her voice was so faint that it took me a few minutes to digest what she said. Once I had collected my thoughts, I posed another question.

"...Since when?"

"Since six hours and thirteen minutes ago by my internal clock."

That number didn't mean much when I'd lost my sense of time.

"Since the moment we were caught in the blizzard."

Her black eyes were calm as always. But my heart was unable to stay calm at this point.

"Why didn't you tell us, then?"

I wasn't trying to blame her. Her quiet nature was proof that she was behaving normally. Something that can't be changed and absolutely must not be changed.

"Which means that we aren't in the real world right now? It's not just this mansion...the snowy mountain area we were walking through that entire time was part of this alternate space that somebody created?"

Nagato was silent for a few moments before responding.

"I do not know."

She lowered her head in a gesture that somehow felt lonely. The sight reminded me of the Nagato from a while back. Made my heart jump for a second. Still, I didn't expect to run into a non-Haruhi-related phenomenon that Nagato couldn't comprehend.

I looked up at the ceiling as I directed my next question to the other SOS Brigade member here.

"What about you? Got anything to say?"

"You can't possibly expect me to understand an anomaly that baffles Nagato."

The deputy brigade chief directed a meaningful glance at Nagato as he straightened his posture.

"All I know is that we aren't in closed space this time. This area was not created by Suzumiya's subconscious."

You sure about that?

"Yes. I happen to be a specialist when it comes to Suzumiya's mental activity. I can tell when she alters reality. Suzumiya has done nothing of the sort this time. She did not desire this situation. I can guarantee that she is in no way responsible for our current predicament. I'm willing to bet on it. I'll double any wager you make."

"Who's responsible then?"

A slight chill ran down my back. Maybe it was the blizzard, but when I looked out the dining hall window, all I could see was gray. I wouldn't be surprised to see one of those pale <Celestials> pop out.

Koizumi apparently took his cue from Nagato as he shrugged in silence. He didn't seem very worried, but that may have been an act. He probably didn't want to let us see him with a grim look on his face.

"Sorry about the wait!"

That was when Haruhi and Asahina walked over carrying a large platter of sandwiches.

According to my internal clock, Haruhi and Asahina had only been gone for a few minutes. We'd only been waiting for five minutes or so at most. However, I asked Haruhi in passing to learn that it'd taken them at least half an hour to prepare the food, which made sense when you looked at the stack of sandwiches they had made. Thin slices of bread that had been toasted individually, seasoned ham and lettuce, chopped-up hard-boiled eggs with mayonnaise. The prep work would have taken much longer than five minutes by itself. And it would have taken a considerable amount of time to prepare so many sandwiches, even if they had used every shortcut in the book. The sandwiches were delicious, but I digress. I'd had the opportunity to experience Haruhi's cooking skills in the form of the Christmas hot pot, but seriously, was there anything she couldn't do? If I'd gone to the same grade school as her, ethics would have been the only subject where I would have had a chance at beating her...

I poked myself in the head.

This wasn't the time to let my mind wander. I needed to focus on our current situation right now.

Asahina seemed rather anxious about the sandwiches she had made, as she would stop breathing every time I reached for another one before sighing in relief or tensing up. The former reaction meant I was grabbing one of Haruhi's and the latter reaction meant I was grabbing one of Asahina's. Very easy to understand.

She still didn't know. I haven't told Koizumi either. And I couldn't let Haruhi find out.

Nagato and I were the only ones who knew that I still had a task to perform.

That's right—

I still needed to go back in time and save the world.

I figured there was no rush, so I was planning on putting it off till next year. Was it a mistake to relax and enjoy the end of this year, considering that I still needed to tell Asahina everything and work out a plan? What if we never got out of this mansion...?

No, wait.

That wouldn't make sense. Nagato, Asahina, and I were guaranteed to travel back in time to the middle of December. Or you wouldn't be able to explain the three figures I saw. Which meant that we would successfully make our way back to normal space? If so, I could finally have some peace of mind.

"Come on, eat up."

Haruhi was stuffing her mouth with sandwiches and gulping down tea.

"There's plenty more left. We can even make more, if you want. The pantry is loaded with food."

Koizumi smiled and winced as he took a bite of his ham cutlet sandwich.

"They're delicious. Absolutely scrumptious. As good as the ones you would find in a restaurant."

His exaggerated compliments were directed at Haruhi, but he wasn't my concern right now. Neither was Asahina, who was barely eating anything because of her guilt about using the kitchen and pantry without permission.

"…"

It was Nagato.

Typically she wouldn't be nibbling away at her food.

The alien-made organic android's hands and mouth were moving at half-speed, as if she had lost her robust appetite.

The light meal was eventually devoured, mostly thanks to Haruhi and my willpower.

"Time to take a bath."

Haruhi made a rather insolent suggestion, but nobody objected. And, by nature, she took the absence of dissent to mean approval.

"We passed that huge bath earlier. There weren't separate ones for each gender so we'll have to take turns, of course. As the brigade chief, I cannot tolerate any inappropriate conduct. Everybody okay with ladies first?"

It probably didn't help that I didn't have any better ideas myself, but I had to appreciate having Haruhi here to rattle off orders every step of the way in situations like this one. That by itself was enough to help provide a distraction. Since I wasn't getting anywhere by sitting around and thinking, moving my body around mechanically might help stimulate the brain and spark some kind of inspiration. Time to trust my brainpower.

"But first, we should decide on room arrangements. Any preferences? They're all the same, though."

According to Koizumi's theory, it would be best for us to stay in the same room, but that suggestion would probably bring a Frog Jump uppercut flying into my face, so I resisted making it.

"We should all take rooms that are next to one another. Just find five rooms that are next to or across from one another."

As soon as I finished that serious spiel, Haruhi stood up from her seat.

"Well, let's find some rooms on the second floor, then."

Haruhi made a dashing figure as she marched off with the rest of us following her. On the way we picked up the skiwear we had left by the entrance and threw everything into the dryer in the laundry room before we went upstairs.

Haruhi chose to commandeer the five rooms that were closest to the stairs so we would be prepared to jump out if anybody returned to the mansion. Koizumi and I were next to each other while Nagato, Haruhi, and Asahina were across the hallway. Haruhi's room was directly across from mine.

As I had noticed when Haruhi and I were walking around the mansion, the bedrooms were literally just that, a bed and not much else in terms of furniture. Those super-cheap business hotels had more furnishings than these bedrooms. Aside from the antique dressing table, there was just a bed and some curtains. The windows were completely sealed shut and on closer inspection turned out to be double-paned. They must have provided some soundproofing effect, as the terrible weather continued outside but I couldn't hear the howling wind or blowing snow. It was actually kind of creepy.

There was nothing to unpack, so once we finished assigning rooms we assembled in the red-carpeted hallway.

Haruhi's smile was unnecessarily suggestive.

"Understand, Kyon?"

Understand what?

"That should be obvious. You aren't allowed to do what the typical adolescent boy would do in this situation. I absolutely hate stereotypes!"

So what am I supposed to do?

"Like I'm saying…"

Haruhi tugged on the arms of the two female brigade members as she leaned into the hair framing Nagato's tranquil face before yelling at me.

"No peeking!"

I watched as the three girls walked away, with Haruhi making all the noise, before slipping out of my own room. There was complete silence in the hallways of the mansion, in contrast to the howling of the blizzard outside. The air was warm. However, I felt anything but comfortable. It was hard to appreciate warmth that only served to chill my heart.

I tiptoed my way over to the room next door and knocked softly.

"What is it?"

Koizumi stuck out his head and greeted me with a warm smile as he opened his mouth to speak. I placed a finger on my lips and he closed his mouth with a knowing look as I quietly slid into his room. I would have preferred to sneak into Asahina's room, but I didn't have time to play around right now.

"I have something to tell you."

"Oh?"

Koizumi sat down on the bed and motioned for me to join him.

"What might that be? I'm very curious. Is this something you don't want the other three members to hear about?"

"I don't care if Nagato hears about this."

I shouldn't need to explain what I'm about to say.

The entire course of events from the disappearance of Haruhi to the moment I woke up in a hospital bed. Ryoko Asakura's return, my second trip through time to the Tanabata three years before, the SOS Brigade members with completely different backgrounds, the adult version of Asahina, and how I was supposed to restore the world in the near future—

"This will be a long story."

I sat down next to Koizumi and began to talk.

Koizumi was an excellent listener, giving appropriate responses at intervals and paying close attention to the very end.

I only covered the major points, so it didn't take as long as I'd expected. There were a few places where I wanted to go into further detail, but my focus was on making my explanation simple and sweeping.

Koizumi willingly listened until the very end.

"I see."

He didn't seem particularly excited as he brushed his fingers against his mouth.

"If what you say is true, I can only say that I find it fascinating."

Is "fascinating" how you talk to people?

"No, I truly feel that way. In fact, I have my own suspicions. Your anecdote would serve to reinforce those suspicions."

I probably didn't have a very amused look on my face. What kind of suspicions are we talking about?

"There is a possibility of decay."

What are you talking about?

"Suzumiya's power. As well as Nagato's ability to manipulate data."

What are you trying to say? I looked at Koizumi. He still had that innocent smile on his face.

"I mentioned before Christmas that Suzumiya has been creating closed space at a less frequent pace. And accordingly, it feels that Nagato…how should I put this, her alien aura? That atmosphere about her. It has been weakening."

"…Heh."

"Suzumiya's behavior is gradually approaching that of an ordinary young girl. On top of that, Nagato is seemingly distancing herself from her position as a terminal for the Data Overmind—at least, that is how it appears to me."

Koizumi looked straight at me.

"As far as I am concerned, these changes are more than I could ever have hoped for. If Suzumiya can accept her current reality and abandon her desire to change the world, my job will more or less be done. And it would be a big help if Nagato were to become an ordinary girl in high school. As for Asahina…well, I suppose we can cope with her being a time traveler."

Koizumi continued with his monologue as if I weren't there.

"You must travel back to the past in order to restore yourself and the world. Because you already witnessed the future versions of you, Nagato, and Asahina at that point in the past—I believe?"

Got that right.

"However, we are currently stranded in the middle of a blizzard on this mountain inside this dubious mansion that someone prepared for us. Circumstances beyond Nagato's comprehension. You could say that we have been trapped inside an alternate space. If the current situation doesn't change, you won't be able to return to the past, so it would be safe to assume that you, Nagato, and Asahina will need to return to our original space at the very least. No, your return is inevitable at this point…"

Wouldn't make sense otherwise. That was probably why I wasn't as nervous as I should have been. I definitely heard my own voice back then. I had yet to return to the past, which meant that I would be making a journey in the near future. In that case, it wouldn't be possible for me to stay in this mansion forever, as it had already been determined that I would have to leave eventually. As Asahina (Big) once said, "Or you wouldn't be here right now, would you?"

"I see."

Koizumi repeated himself as he smiled at me.

"However, I have a different theory to offer. A rather pessimistic theory, if you will. Put simply, this hypothesis assumes that it won't matter if none of us ever return to our original space."

Stop trying to act smart and just spit it out.

"Well then," Koizumi began as he lowered his voice cautiously.

"It is possible that we are not the originals but mere copies in an alternate world."

He paused to let me absorb his words, but they made no sense at all.

"Let me try to make this easier to understand. For instance, if our minds were scanned and copied into a digital space, what would happen? Our minds and nothing else were transported to a virtual space."

"Copies?"

"Yes. This isn't limited to our minds. Anything is possible if we're dealing with power on the level of the Data Overmind. In other words, we who have wandered into this alternate space are not the originals but faithful copies that were created at a certain point. The originals are...well, they may be partying at Tsuruya's vacation home as we speak."

Hold on. Am I having trouble understanding your reasoning because I'm unlearned?

"That shouldn't be the case, but I will try to use a more relevant example. Let us pretend that you are playing a computer game. A fantasy RPG. When you're about to venture into a cave with no idea what may be inside, you save first to be safe, naturally. Even if your entire party is wiped out, you can reload from that save point. As long as the copied data exists, the originals may be kept in a safe place while all risk is delegated to the copies. If anything goes wrong, you simply reset. What would happen if that applied to our current situation?"

Koizumi had a resigned look on his face, but his smile was still intact.

"In other words, we are copies, mere guinea pigs, that have been placed in this simulated space constructed by some unknown character. A place created for the sole purpose of observing our reaction to these circumstances."

"Koizumi…"

As I spoke, I was suddenly hit by a violent sense of déjà vu. The same incoherent intrusion by a fragment of memory I had experienced last summer during that endless August. What is this? A memory I have no recollection of is screaming in a corner of my mind. To remember.

I spoke hesitantly.

"Has anything like this happened before?"

"Do I recall being stranded on a snowy mountain before? No, I do not."

"That's not what I meant."

It had nothing to do with being on a snowy mountain. I could vaguely recall being trapped in a different dimension…for some odd reason. In a very surreal place…

"You mean during the cave cricket extermination? We were certainly in an alternate space at the time."

"Not that either."

I racked my brain for an answer. All I could come up with was an image of Koizumi dressed in odd clothing along with Haruhi, Nagato, Asahina, and me.

Yeah, Koizumi. For some reason, I have this feeling that you were holding a harp. All of us were in archaic dress and focused on some task…

"You couldn't be referring to memories from a past life? I would expect you to be the last person to suggest such an idea."

If humans could actually remember past lives, we would all get along a lot better. Except that's just an excuse used by the people who have a problem with the present.

"You are absolutely correct."

Damn it. I can't remember. My mind is telling me that I have no such memories of alternate space. However, deep down, my senses are saying otherwise.

What was it? I could only think of fragmented keywords such as "king," "pirates," "spaceships," and "gunfights." What did this mean? My memory was telling me that nothing like that ever happened. There was a piece of the puzzle deep down in my heart that just didn't fit. But I wasn't able to identify it.

Koizumi must have seen the frustrated look on my face as he continued in a composed voice.

"If we are in a space that cannot be deciphered by Nagato and causes her strain, we should be able to deduce the identity of the party or parties responsible for our mountain ordeal, the blizzard, and this mansion as well."

I didn't say a word.

"An entity with as much power as Nagato, or more."

Who would that be?

"I don't know. However, if I were the one responsible, I would have dealt with Nagato first. Unlike Asahina and me, who are virtually powerless alone, Nagato is directly connected to the Data Overmind."

Since it seemed more godlike than Haruhi. Though I wasn't entirely sure if the Data Overmind was one or many. But Nagato had already confessed that her link with her boss had been severed.

"It's possible that we are dealing with a creature that wields more power than Nagato's creator. Though that would effectively eliminate us from the picture…"

The handsome freak apparently thought of something, as he broke off in the middle of his sentence and crossed his arms.

"So you know Ryoko Asakura?"

I'd almost forgotten about her, but certain events this month have ensured that I will never forget her.

"What if the radical faction, a minority within the Data Overmind, succeeded in achieving a coup d'état? They may as well be gods from our perspective. It would be very simple to trap us in a different dimension once Nagato had been isolated."

I remembered. The affable and cheerful class representative. The edge of the sharp knife. I had been attacked by Asakura twice and saved by Nagato both times.

"Whatever the case, there is no change in the outcome. We will spend all eternity in this mansion, unable to escape."

Like the mythical Dragon Palace?

"A very apt metaphor. We have received a warm reception, one might say. Every possible need has been provided for. A warm and spacious mansion with a stocked refrigerator, a large bath with hot water, comfortable bedrooms…Everything besides a means of escape from the mansion itself."

Pretty pointless then. I hadn't given up on my life to the point where I would want to idle away in this unknown space forever. It was too early to end my high school experience, before a year had passed. And there were other people I wanted to see again who weren't here with us. Taniguchi and Kunikida would be included among them, and it'd be pretty sad if I never saw my family or Shamisen again. Besides, I hated winter. No offense to the people who live in Iceland, but I could spend the rest of my life surrounded by snow and ice and never get used to it.

You can call me the man who loves summer heat and cicada sounds.

"I am relieved to hear you say that."

Koizumi sighed with an exaggerated gesture.

"If Suzumiya notices this abnormal situation and unleashes her power, nobody can guess what the outcome will be. That may actually be the goal of the person or persons who set this up. Since there have barely been any developments to speak of as of late, they are attempting to stimulate her into a reaction of some sort. A very common tactic. If we are mere copies that have been detached from the originals and placed in a simulated space, there is no need to hold back. You wouldn't feel bad about making a game character suffer, would you?"

When you put it that way, I can't deny that I'm guilty of committing a similar offense in the past. However, game characters are merely data, while we exist as flesh and blood.

"First, we must escape this place. We would be safer stranded in the real world than trapped in this alternate space. I'm sure that we'll find a way. No, we absolutely have to find a way. Any existence that seeks to trap Suzumiya and the rest of us in here is clearly an enemy. And not an enemy of the "Agency" or Data Overmind, but an enemy of the SOS Brigade."

Whatever. I'm willing to take anybody who agrees with me.

After that, I began to think long and hard, and I was joined by Koizumi, who placed his hand on his chin in a pose of contemplation.

Eventually—

A soft knock shattered the silence between Koizumi and me. I stood up stiffly as though my body had been glued to the bed and opened the door.

"Um...The bath is free now. Please take your turn."

Asahina, fresh out of the bath, was flushed in the face in a rather sweet and innocent display of sensuality. A strand of damp hair clung to her cheek almost provocatively while her exposed legs, extending from the long T-shirt she wore, were absolutely captivating. If I had been in a normal state of mind, I would have immediately swept her off her feet and taken her off to the corner of my room.

"Where are Haruhi and Nagato?"

I looked down the hallway as I spoke, and Asahina giggled.

"They're drinking juice in the dining hall."

She must have sensed my penetrating gaze, as she tugged on the hem of her T-shirt in a fluster.

"Ah, you'll find a change of clothes outside the bath. That's where I got this shirt. There were also bath towels and other stuff like shampoo…"

It was impossible to describe how lovely she looked as she timidly spoke.

I turned back to Koizumi and gave him a look to stop him in his tracks before quickly moving into the hallway and closing the door behind me.

"Asahina, I have a question for you."

"Yes?"

She looked up at me all goggle-eyed as she cocked her head uncertainly.

"How do you feel about this mansion? I find it incredibly unnatural, but I'd like to know your opinion."

Asahina batted her long and beautiful eyelashes.

"Well, Suzumiya thinks that this might be…um, foreshadowing? For the mystery game Koizumi prepared. At least, that's what she said…when we were taking a bath."

I was fine with Haruhi jumping to her own conclusions, but I needed Asahina to stay alert.

"How would you explain the irregular flow of time? You witnessed Koizumi's experiment, right?"

"Yes. But that was part of the gimmick…? Wasn't it?"

I pressed one hand against my forehead as I tried to suppress a sigh. I had no idea how Koizumi could possibly pull that off, and even if this was just a trick to fool us, it wouldn't be fair of him to hide that fact from Haruhi. Besides, doesn't Asahina specialize in issues related to time?

I decided to go for it.

"Asahina, could you try to contact the future? Right now, right here."

"Huh?"

The baby-faced upperclassman looked at me in surprise.

"I can't talk to you about that. Hee hee hee. It's classified information—"

She burst into laughter, but I wasn't joking around or trying to be funny.

However, Asahina continued to giggle.

"Come on. Go take your bath before Suzumiya gets mad. Hee hee hee."

And with that, the petite upperclassman turned and flitted toward the staircase like a butterfly fluttering around a field of flowers in spring, turning back once to send me an awkward wink before disappearing down the stairs.

No good. I can't count on Asahina. That only leaves…

"Damn."

I stared at the carpet and sighed.

I didn't want to put any more strain on her. And yet, she was the only one capable of doing something about our current predicament. Koizumi was all talk and conjecture, and if somebody rubbed Haruhi the wrong way she might blow up on us. I still had an ace up my sleeve, sure, but after hearing Koizumi's spiel, I wasn't about to carelessly put it into play. That might be the goal of whoever it was who drove us into this situation.

"What am I supposed to do…?"

*　　　*　　　*

I was hoping that a bath might help my circulation and provide the inspiration I needed for a brilliant idea, but I was fully aware of the limitations of my brain and its inability to produce an idea that would improve our situation. It was kind of pathetic how I didn't even feel disappointed by the obvious result.

As Asahina said, there were bath towels and a change of clothes outside the bath. Neatly folded T-shirts of every size and jersey pants hanging from the rack. I chose a set of clothes at random before joining Koizumi in heading to the dining hall.

The three girls who had gone before us were setting bottles of juice on the table.

"That was a long bath. What were you doing?"

I'm pretty sure that I barely took longer than a crow would to bathe.

Haruhi handed me some orange juice, which I drank as I glanced between Nagato and the window. Haruhi was in a much better mood after warming up her body as she chugged her bottle of juice with a grin on her face. Asahina was smiling like she didn't realize the predicament we were in. Nagato looked even smaller than usual, but that may have just been an effect of her damp hair hanging down.

Anyway, what time was it? I looked out the window, but all I could see was snow flying around. Still, it wasn't very bright outside. But the fact that it wasn't completely dark only added to the creepy atmosphere.

It seemed that Haruhi had also lost her sense of time—

"Let's go play around in the rec room?"

—As she was suggesting that we seek entertainment.

"Karaoke's fine, but it's been a while since I've played mah-jongg. Bets will be pegged to the scoring and anything goes as far as rules are concerned. But I want to focus on building good hands so none of that bonus stuff is allowed. Double points for thirteen orphans and four concealed triplets, okay?"

I had no intention of getting picky about the rules, but I shook my head slowly. Right now we didn't have time for karaoke or mah-jongg. We needed to brainstorm.

"Let's get some sleep for now. We'll have plenty of time to party later on. I'm pretty tired."

We'd been trudging around with our skis for hours, half covered in snow. Haruhi would be the only one whose muscles weren't fatigued after that excursion.

"That's true…"

Haruhi looked around at each individual face to gauge everyone's opinion.

"Well, I guess it's okay. Let's rest a bit. But when we wake up, we're going to party hard."

Her eyes were shining bright enough for two or three spiral nebulas.

Once we withdrew to our respective rooms, I plopped down on the bed and held a little conference in my head. However, these situations are when a person's incompetence tends to be exposed, and I was unable to produce a single useful plan. The minutes ticked by as I lay on the bed in total silence, hoping that someone would say something, and I must have dozed off at some point, for I heard a voice.

"Kyon."

Someone suddenly called my name, which made me jump up.

I hadn't heard the door open or the sound of footsteps or rustling clothes that would be associated with someone's entering the room. I hadn't even sensed that there was another person there. Which meant that I was already surprised to begin with when I looked at the shadow standing in the middle of the room and doubled over in shock.

"Asahina?"

The only light in the room came from the window, curtains drawn aside, which was tinted by the snow. However, despite the dim lighting, it would have been impossible for me to be mistaken. It was Asahina, the SOS Brigade mascot who graced the clubroom with her presence like an adorable little fairy.

"Kyon…"

Asahina repeated herself as she smiled at me and hesitantly walked over to me. I sat back down on the bed in a hurry as she took a seat next to me with her legs exposed. There was something out of place that I couldn't put my finger on, and then I noticed that she wasn't wearing the same clothes as when she'd said good night in the hallway. She was no longer dressed in a long T-shirt. But she was still barely dressed.

Asahina was looking up at me, wearing only a white shirt, in a scene that could have come straight out of somebody's fantasy. From an extremely close position.

"Say…"

Her lovely childlike face was contorted in a look of supplication.

"May I sleep here?"

A question that almost made my lungs jump out of my mouth. (This is weird.)

Her misty eyes looked straight at my face and her cheeks were flushed. Asahina slowly leaned against my arm. (What is this?)

"I'm afraid of being in a room by myself. I can't fall asleep…If I'm by your side, I should be able to rest comfortably…"

I could feel her body heat through the flimsy shirt. It was so hot that I almost thought I was on fire. Something soft pressed against me. Asahina was hugging my arm as her face drew near.

"May I? Okay?"

A rhetorical question. No male or female could ever possibly refuse such a request when it came from Asahina. So it's okay. I mean, this bed is too big for one person…(Hold on.)

She giggled and released my arm with a smile as she began to unbutton her shirt, which was already half-open to begin with, deliberately exposing soft curves that made my head spin. The same cleavage I had seen when I accidentally opened the door while Haruhi was putting Asahina into a bunny outfit, in the photographs that were slumbering in a hidden folder on the hard drive of our computer. (Wake up. You've got it wrong.)

Only two buttons remained fastened on her white shirt…no, make that one. This was more erotic than if she'd been completely naked. Since we were dealing with a quality model here. After all, this was Asahina. (Hey.)

Asahina looked up at me with upturned eyes as she flashed a shy and seductive smile. Her fingers lingered on the last button. I should avert my eyes. (Look closer.)

Her shirt was essentially split down the middle to reveal pale skin that rose and fell with each breath. A scene that was just as artistic as Venus on a shell (You're doing it wrong.) with one side of her glistening bosom (That's more like it.) adorned by a star-shaped…

I suddenly sucked in a deep breath.

"Grr…!"

I jumped away from the bed like a loaded spring.

"No!"

Take a closer look. How did I not notice? The method of verifying Asahina's identity that I knew best. I used it just the other day. If I checked a certain spot on Asahina's body, I would know.

"Who are you?"

—This Asahina didn't have a mole on her left breast.

The half-naked girl looked up at me in distress.

"Why? Are you rejecting me?"

What if this was the real Asahina? (I already said that you're wrong.) Would I still have been able to keep a firm grip on my libido? No, forget that. That wasn't the issue here. Asahina would never sneak into my room to seduce me. She didn't need to.

"You aren't Asahina."

I slowly inched backward as I stared at the tears welling up in those gorgeous eyes. Something's wrong with me. Does it really matter if she's Asahina or not when I'm making her look so sad? (Stop that.)

"Enough of that."

I managed to get the words out of my mouth.

"Who are you? The person who made this mansion? Are you an alien or a slider? Why are you doing this?"

"...Kyon-kun."

This Asahina's voice was oozing with sorrow. She looked down and bit her lip before taking action.

"!"

Her shirt fluttered in the air as she raced for the door like the wind. She paused for a moment in the doorway and turned to me with teary eyes before dashing out into the hallway. The door slammed shut with a surprisingly loud sound that woke me up as I remembered that the door had been locked from the inside. It should have been impossible for anybody to get in without a spare key.

"Please wait!"

I yelled out in a polite voice as I ran over to the door and threw it open.

Bam. Another loud sound. I certainly used a considerable amount of force, but opening a single door shouldn't produce that much noise—

"Huh? You..."

Haruhi's face was right in front of mine. Haruhi, in the room across the hall, had opened her own door at the same time and stuck her head out as she stared at me with her jaw dropped.

"Kyon, weren't you in my room a second ago…or I guess not."

Haruhi and I weren't the only ones sticking our heads out in the hallway.

"Um."

Asahina, wearing a T-shirt, was to Haruhi's right as she stuck her puzzled face through a half-open door. On the opposite side—

"…"

—was Nagato's slim figure. I also looked to my side.

"Well, well."

Koizumi was scratching his nose as he gave me an odd look and smiled awkwardly.

That explained the loud sound at least. The five of us had opened our doors at virtually the same time. A quintet in unison, if you will.

"What's up with everybody?"

Haruhi was the first to recover and glare at me.

"Why did everybody come out of their room at the same time?"

I was chasing a fake Asahina—or so I was going to say when I realized that Haruhi had said something rather odd.

"What about you? Were you going to the bathroom or something?"

Surprisingly enough, Haruhi looked down at the floor and bit her lip before she finally responded.

"I had a weird dream. A dream where you snuck into my room. You were talking and, um, acting completely out of character so I knew that something was wrong…Yeah, I punched you in the face and you ran away…Huh? It was just a dream…right? But something doesn't seem quite right."

If that had just been a dream, it would mean you're still dreaming at this very moment. I watched as Haruhi's brow creased and Koizumi walked over to me.

"I had a similar experience."

He stared at my face.

"You also appeared in my room. At least, someone who matched you perfectly in outward appearance. However, the person who resembled you was behaving in a rather uncomfortable manner... Well, let's just say that he did some things I would never expect you to do, yes?"

I was getting scared for no real reason. I looked away from Koizumi's smirking face and focused my attention on Asahina. The real one. I could tell instantly. How could I have been fooled by that phony? Behavior, general aura, you name it. This was how Asahina was supposed to be.

I'm not sure how Asahina interpreted my gaze, as she suddenly blushed. I was about to ask if I had also shown up in her room.

"Suzumiya came to me."

She twisted her fingers together.

"Um, a Suzumiya that was kind of strange... I'm not sure how to say this, but she almost seemed like an imposter..."

It was an imposter. That was clear, but what was going on here exactly? Each of us had a fake member show up in our room? Asahina in my room, me in Haruhi and Koizumi's room, Haruhi in Asahina's room...

"Nagato," I said before asking, "who came to your room?"

Nagato, dressed only in a T-shirt like Asahina, silently looked up at me with a seemingly numb expression on her face.

"You."

She responded in a barely audible voice before slowly closing her eyes.

And then—

"...Yuki?!"

—Haruhi exclaimed in the background as I witnessed an unbelievable sight.

Nagato, the one and only Yuki Nagato, collapsed in a heap as if an invisible hand had pushed her down.

"What's wrong, Yuki? Hey…"

Every one of us was left dumbstruck, with the exception of Haruhi, who immediately ran over to support Nagato's small frame.

"Whoa…She's burning up. Yuki, you okay? Hey, Yuki!"

Nagato's eyes were still shut and her head was limp. Her expressionless face suggested that she was asleep. However, I had a gut feeling that Nagato wasn't simply slumbering away.

Haruhi put her arm around Nagato's shoulder as she started to bark out orders with a stern look on her face.

"Koizumi, carry Yuki to her bed. Kyon, go find some ice bags. There should be some around there somewhere. Mikuru, go wet a few towels."

Asahina, Koizumi, and I stood there gaping for a moment before Haruhi yelled at us again.

"Hurry!"

Once I saw Koizumi lift up the unconscious Nagato, I quickly headed down the stairs. Ice bags, huh? Where am I supposed to look…

That particular line of thought was probably a sign that I hadn't recovered from the shock of seeing Nagato collapse. I still couldn't believe what had happened. As a result, I could no longer be bothered to care about the mystery surrounding the fake Asahina in my room or the phonies that had appeared in the other rooms. Do whatever you want. It's got nothing to do with me.

"Balls."

We were seriously in trouble. Damn, I'd been hoping to let Nagato enjoy a normal and peaceful life for a while, but this would be the exact opposite.

As I wandered around without any idea of where to find any ice bags, I somehow ended up in the kitchen. In my house, we kept the cooling sheets in the fridge instead of the first-aid box. Was that the case in this mansion?

"Wait."

I froze as I was about to grab the handle of the large refrigerator. I visualized an ice bag and concentrated as hard as I could.

Then I opened the fridge.

"...Knew it."

A blue ice bag rested on top of a head of cabbage.

How considerate of them. A very convenient mechanism. But it was having the opposite effect—that of strengthening my resolve.

That we couldn't stay here another second.

I left the dining hall with the chilly ice bag in my hand when I saw Koizumi standing by the entrance to the mansion. He was staring at the door, but I wasn't sure why. Did Haruhi order him to gather snow or something?

I walked over to offer a few words of candid advice, but Koizumi noticed me and spoke first.

"Perfect timing. Could you take a look at this?"

He pointed at the door.

I saved my own remarks for later and looked in the direction he was pointing to discover something so strange that I was left speechless.

"What is this?"

Those were the only words I could manage.

"I didn't notice this here earlier."

"Yes, it wasn't here before. I was the last person to enter the mansion. I checked the door when I shut it and this wasn't there at the time."

An object that was difficult to describe had been attached to the inside of the front door of the mansion. I guess the closest comparison would be something along the lines of a console or panel.

A shiny metal plate—or I guess that "panel" would be the most appropriate word here—around twenty inches long on each side was affixed to the wooden door, sporting symbols and numbers that made my head hurt.

I sucked it up and focused my eyes. First, at the very top:

$$x - y = (D - 1) - z$$

And then a little below that:

$$x = \square, y = \square, z = \square$$

The boxes were actually indentations, as if we were supposed to place something in them. I stared at the three holes in bewilderment.

"The pieces are over there."

Koizumi pointed at the floor, where there was a wooden box with an assortment of numbered blocks inside. On closer look, there were three sets of blocks numbered 0 through 9. I picked one up. It was shaped like a mah-jongg tile and was about the same weight. However, the difference was that the surfaces of these tiles were engraved with Arabic numerals.

Blocks for the ten different digits with three of each, all stored in the flat wooden box.

"The numbers that correspond to the solution for this equation," Koizumi said as he picked up a block and examined it, "should be placed in the open spaces, I presume."

I looked back at the formula again. My head began to hurt. Math was one of the many subjects that gave me considerable trouble.

"Koizumi, do you know the answer?"

"I believe that I have seen a similar problem before, but I'll need more information before I can try to solve it. If the goal is to simply make both sides of the equation equal, there are a multitude of possible combinations. But if this puzzle only has one correct solution, we will need additional conditions before we can settle on an answer."

I turned my attention to the letter in the equation that didn't quite fit.

"What's with the D? It looks like we aren't required to solve for it."

"And it's the only letter that's uppercase."

Koizumi toyed with a number 0 tile as he lowered his voice.

"This formula...I have a feeling that I recognize it. It's on the tip of my tongue...What was it? I'm pretty sure that I saw this recently."

He stood in place with his brow creased. That's unusual. You rarely ever see Koizumi with a serious look on his face, deep in thought.

"So, is this supposed to mean something?"

I returned the tile in my hand to the box.

"I can see that a math problem suddenly popped up on the inside of the door, but why does it matter?"

"Yes."

Koizumi seemed to snap out of it.

"It's the key. The door has been locked. There is no way to open it from the inside. I spent some time fiddling with the doorknob to no avail."

"What?"

"You'll understand once you give it a try. As you can see, there is no keyhole or lock on the inside."

I gave it a try. The door wouldn't open.

"Who locked the door and how? If this is an automatic lock, we should be able to open the door from the inside."

"More proof that common sense does not apply in this space."

Koizumi went back to his mindless smile.

"I do not know who is responsible, but someone is trying to trap us in here. The windows have all been sealed shut and the door at the entrance is locked tight …"

"So, what about the formula on the panel? A quiz for killing time?"

"If I'm not mistaken, this formula is the key to opening the door."

Koizumi sounded rather calm.

"Our only means of escape, provided to us by Nagato."

Koizumi paid no heed to the rush of nostalgia I was experiencing after recent memories had resurfaced as he continued to rattle away.

"You could call this a war of data. A form of limited conflict, if you will. Someone has trapped us within this alternate space. Nagato has countered by providing us with a means of escape. I assume that this formula would be the result. If we solve this equation, we will be able to return to our original dimension. If we fail, we'll be stuck here. Simple as that."

Koizumi rapped on the door.

"We have no way of knowing the basic details of this war. As this is a war of data between elemental entities, it is beyond our understanding. However, their struggle is manifested through such practical measures. This panel would be one such example."

A math problem didn't seem to fit in with this bizarre mansion.

"This is no coincidence. Each of us experienced a rather peculiar dream, which was immediately followed by Nagato's collapse and the appearance of this panel on the door… This sequence of events did not occur by accident. They must be related somehow."

If Koizumi was worried in any way, he was doing a good job of hiding it.

"I am positive that this is the key to our escape. Most likely courtesy of Nagato."

I checked to see if it said COPYRIGHT © BY YUKI NAGATO on the panel anywhere. It didn't.

"This is merely conjecture, but I believe that Nagato's power is limited in this space. Now that her link with the Data Overmind has been severed, she can only rely on her innate abilities. That would explain the haphazard means of escape."

You're making a lot of sense for mere conjecture.

"Yes, I suppose. The 'Agency' has made contact with other interfaces aside from Nagato, so I happen to have access to certain information."

I was interested in hearing about these other aliens, but there wasn't time for that right now. We needed to deal with this weird puzzle first. I was looking between the symbols on the panel and the numbered blocks in the wooden box when I remembered something Nagato had said in her flat voice.

"This space is putting strain on me."

I didn't know the identity of the person who had led us into this mansion in the middle of a blizzard, but I wasn't going to forgive whoever was responsible for Nagato's getting a fever and passing out. I wasn't about to go along with that little puke's plans. I was ready to do whatever it took to get out of this place and back to Tsuruya's vacation home. Accompanied by every single SOS Brigade member, no exceptions.

Nagato had done her job. I couldn't see or hear her handiwork, but I was certain that she'd been fighting this invisible "enemy" from the second we stepped into this alternate space. That was probably why she looked more out of it than usual. As a result, she was able to create this small opening as she collapsed. Now it was our turn to open the door.

"Let's bust out of this joint."

Koizumi responded to my proclamation with an easy smile.

"Of course, that was the plan. This place may be comfortable, but I wouldn't want to stay here forever. Utopia and dystopia are merely two sides of the same coin."

"Koizumi."

My voice was so serious that I surprised myself.

"Can you use your ESP to open a hole? The situation's looking bad. With Nagato the way she is now, you're the only one who can do something about this."

"You are overestimating my abilities."

Koizumi was still smiling, despite our current predicament.

"I do not recall ever saying that I am an omnipotent esper. My powers only come into play under certain conditions. You should be aware of that fact by—"

I didn't bother listening to the rest of his sentence. I grabbed Koizumi by the collar and pulled him over to me.

"I didn't ask for your excuses."

I glared at Koizumi and that cynical smile of his.

"Don't you specialize in alternate space? Asahina can't be depended on, and Haruhi's out of the question. There must be something you can do, like with the cave cricket. Or is your 'Agency' made up of a bunch of useless losers?"

I would also be a useless loser in this case. There was nothing I could do. I couldn't even keep my cool, which probably placed me below Koizumi. The only idea I could come up with was to beat the crap out of Koizumi, and then have him beat the crap out of me. Since I wouldn't be able to beat the crap out of myself without holding back.

"What are you doing?"

A sharp, irritated voice stabbed into my back.

"Kyon, what's going on with those ice bags? You were taking forever so I came down to check on you and what? You're sparring with Koizumi? What are you trying to do?"

Haruhi was standing at full height with her hands on her hips. The look on her face reminded me of an old man in my neighborhood who managed to catch a chronic persimmon thief redhanded.

"Could you be more considerate of Yuki? There isn't any time for you to play around!"

If Haruhi was interpreting this exchange between Koizumi and me as "playing around," her mind was clearly elsewhere. I released my grip on Koizumi and picked up the ice bag from the spot on the floor where it had fallen while I wasn't paying attention.

Haruhi quickly took the bag from me.

"What is this?"

Her gaze shifted to the odd equation on the door. Koizumi straightened his collar as he replied.

"Indeed, the two of us were wondering the same thing. Do you have any ideas?"

"Isn't that Euler?"

I was thrown off by Haruhi's instant response. Koizumi continued.

"You mean Leonhard Euler? The mathematician?"

"I don't know his first name."

Koizumi looked back at the puzzle panel on the door for a few seconds.

"I see."

He snapped for dramatic effect.

"Euler's polyhedron theorem. This must be a variation of that. Suzumiya, I am amazed that you were able to recognize this."

"I might be wrong. But the *D* is probably where you put the number of dimensions. I'm guessing."

Let's not worry about whether you're right or wrong. I have a much more obvious question that needs to be answered first. Who is Euler and what did he do? What is a polyhedron theorem? Did we learn about this in math? Though I was hesitant to ask all of these questions, since I was always half-asleep during math class.

"No, this usually doesn't come up in high school math courses. However, I'm sure that you've heard of the Seven Bridges of Königsberg."

That I know. That was one of the puzzles math teacher Yoshizaki mentioned during class. You have two islands connected to the mainland by a number of bridges and you have to cross all of them once and only once? I remember that there isn't a solution.

"Yes." Koizumi nodded. "The problem was originally formed on a flat plane, but Euler proved that it also applied to a three-dimensional plane. He formed a number of famous theorems, and this is one of them."

Koizumi explained.

"His theorem states that when you look at a convex polyhedron and take the number of vertices plus the number of faces minus the number of edges, you will always end up with two."

"..."

Koizumi must have recognized my desire to abandon anything related to math as he smiled wryly and slid one arm behind his back.

"Then I shall use a simple diagram to explain."

He took out a black felt-tip pen. Where'd that come from? Had he been carrying that around on him? Or did he use the same method I had used to obtain the ice bag?

Koizumi knelt down on the floor and began to cheerfully draw on the red carpet. Neither Haruhi nor I even moved to stop him.

In this mansion drawing on the furniture, floors, or walls was clearly not a problem.

Eventually, he produced a picture of a dice-like cube.

"I'm sure that you can see this is a regular hexahedron. There are a total of eight vertices. It has six faces, as the name would tell you. And there are twelve edges. Eight plus six minus twelve equals two...yes?"

Koizumi must have felt that wasn't enough, as he drew a new diagram.

"Now we have a square pyramid. Count and you'll find there are five vertices, five faces, and eight edges. Five plus five minus eight will also yield an answer of two. You could apply this formula to any polyhedron up to a hectohedron with a hundred faces and the answer will always be two. This would be Euler's polyhedron theorem."

"I see. I understand now. But why did Haruhi mention the number of dimensions?"

"That is also quite simple. This polyhedron theorem is not limited to three-dimensional objects, as it can also apply to two-dimensional planes. However, in that case vertices plus faces minus edges will consistently yield an answer of one. This form of the theorem can be applied to the Seven Bridges of Königsberg."

A new doodle appeared on the carpet.

"As you can see, this is a pentagram. A star that can be drawn in one stroke."

I did the counting myself this time. There were one, two...ten vertices. It had...six faces. The number of edges would be the highest at, uh, a total of fifteen. Which would give you the equation ten plus six minus fifteen, and the answer was—one.

By the time I finished running those calculations in my head, Koizumi had finished drawing a fourth diagram. This one looked like a failed attempt at the Big Dipper.

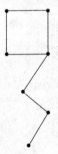

"The theorem also applies to such irregular figures."

I was starting to get sick of this, but I did the math anyway. Uh...seven vertices, one face, and seven edges? I see, you still get one.

Koizumi smiled brightly as he replaced the cap on the felt pen.

"In other words, the answer for a three-dimensional object will equal two and the answer for a two-dimensional plane will equal one. With that in mind, let us return to the formula before us."

He used the pen to point to the panel on the door.

"$X - y = (D - 1) - z$. Let us assume that x refers to the number of vertices. We can then assume that y, the variable being subtracted, is the number of edges. The z, or number of faces, is more difficult to discern, as it was shifted to the right side of the equation and consequently had its sign reversed. As for the $(D - 1)$, the difference should equal two for a polyhedron and one for a flat plane, which means that D would be three when dealing in three dimensions and two when dealing with two dimensions. Thus, the D refers to the number of dimensions. D for 'Dimension.' "

I listened to him in silence and concentrated on thinking. Yeah, I think I more or less understand now. I see. So this is the theorem thing Herr Euler came up with.

"So?"

I posed this question.

"What's the answer to this math quiz? Which numerical blocks do we use for x, y, and z?"

"Well."

Back came Koizumi's answer.

"I don't know. Not without the original polyhedron or plane as a reference."

There's no point, then. Where are we supposed to find the original figure?

Koizumi merely shrugged, which only added to my irritation.

However, that was when something happened.

Haruhi, who had been staring at the equation with a look of concentration on her face, abruptly remembered something else she was supposed to do.

"Forget about this—anyway, Kyon!"

She suddenly yelled at me.

"You need to visit Yuki later."

I was going to do that anyway, but why are you being so high and mighty about it?

"Because she called out your name while she was mumbling. Only once though."

Nagato called out my name? Mumbling?

"What did she say exactly?"

"She just went, 'Kyon.'"

Nagato had never called me by that name before. Hell, I can't recall her ever calling me by my actual name or nickname or any sort of name for that matter. She always addressed me by a second-person pronoun…

I felt this irregular haze of emotion bunch up in my chest.

"No…"

Koizumi voiced an objection.

"Are you sure that she said the word 'Kyon'? Is it possible that you misheard her?"

What's with him? He's going to complain about what Nagato says in her sleep?

However, Koizumi paid me no attention as he looked straight at Haruhi.

"Suzumiya, this is very important. Please try to remember."

Koizumi's tone was so intense that Haruhi appeared to be surprised as her eyes wandered upward while she thought hard.

"Yes. I didn't hear her very clearly, so it might not have been 'Kyon.' And her voice was soft. She could have been saying 'hyon' or 'jyon.' But I'm pretty sure that it wasn't 'kyan' or 'kyun.'"

"I see."

Koizumi looked pleased.

"You're unsure about the first syllable, but you were able to catch the last part. Aha, I see. I'm sure that Nagato wasn't trying to say 'Kyon' or any of those other sounds. She meant to say 'yon,' I believe."

"'Yon'?" I asked.

"Yes, as in the Japanese word for 'four.' "

"What does 'four' have to do with…"

I stopped in the middle of my sentence and looked back up at the formula.

"Hey."

Haruhi's lips were puckered together in irritation.

"We don't have time to waste on this little math quiz. You need to worry about Yuki. Honestly!"

She swung the ice bag around as her eyes narrowed angrily.

"You better come visit her later! Got it?!"

And with that loud cry, she turned and stomped back upstairs. Koizumi watched to make sure that she was out of sight before turning to me with a look of conviction on his face.

"We have been given the required conditions. Now, we can solve for x, y, and z."

"Please think back to the phenomenon we experienced a short while ago. The imposters that Suzumiya dismissed as a dream but that I found to be somewhat realistic."

The felt pen was in Koizumi's hand again as he knelt down.

"Let us draw a diagram that shows which apparition visited each room."

Koizumi started by drawing a dot on the red carpet and labeling it K.

"This represents you. Asahina was the one who visited your room, I believe."

He drew a line straight up from that point and added another dot at the end, which he labeled MA.

"Suzumiya was the one to appear in Asahina's room."

He drew a line from the MA point that went down diagonally to the left, and labeled the new dot HS.

"You were the one who showed up in Suzumiya's room."

He drew a line connecting the HS point with the K point and formed a right triangle.

"And you also appeared in my room. Though I must say that the imposter behaved nothing like you. I seriously doubt you would ever do any of those things, even if you were to go insane."

He drew a line that went down from the K point and added a dot that was labeled IK.

"Nagato mentioned that you were also the one in her room."

I'd already realized what he was doing. He drew a line extending from the point that represented me and labeled the new dot YN before replacing the cap on his pen to signal that he was done.

"They were all related. The imposters that were neither dream nor reality were apparitions Nagato created."

I looked carefully at Koizumi's newest diagram.

A figure four that could be drawn in one stroke.

"We simply need to apply this figure to the formula on the door. A relationship chart that connects us to the fakes we saw. The figure is a flat plane, so D will automatically equal two."

He continued before I had a chance to do the math in my head.

"For this figure, the number of vertices would be the number of members, so five. There is only one face, the triangle formed by you, Suzumiya, and Asahina. There are a total of five edges."

Koizumi brushed aside a bang and smiled.

"X equals five, y equals five, z equals one. That would be the answer. Both sides happen to equal zero."

*　　*　　*

There wasn't any time to be impressed or offer praise.

I picked up the three corresponding numerical blocks. Now that we had established a solution, we needed to quickly apply it.

However, Koizumi apparently still had his doubts.

"I am afraid of the possibility that this is an erase program."

I guess I might as well ask what he's talking about.

"If we are mere copies that only exist within this simulation, there is no need for us to leave this alternate space. The originals already exist in the real world."

Koizumi raised both arms in supplication.

"It is entirely possible that solving this equation will trigger a process that will delete our existences. In other words, we would be committing a form of suicide. Now, would you prefer to live here for an eternity in relative comfort with very little variety, or would you prefer to be deleted?"

I don't like either option. I have no wish to live forever, but I'm also firmly against the idea of ending my life anytime soon. I am my own man. There is no substitute for me.

"I trust Nagato."

My voice was surprisingly calm.

"I also trust you. I believe that your answer is the correct one. However, that trust is limited to your solution to this equation."

"I see."

I had to wonder if Koizumi had mastered the art of telepathy as he smiled gently and took a half step back.

"I shall leave the decision up to you. No matter what happens, I can follow you and Suzumiya. After all, it's my job and my duty."

Good thing that you seem to be enjoying yourself then. It's hard to find a job that's actually fun.

Koizumi's smile became a little more serious.

"Assuming that we are able to return to ordinary space, I have a promise I would like to make."

He almost sounded at peace.

"If a situation should ever arise where Nagato is in a great deal of trouble and that situation is beneficial to the 'Agency,' I will betray the 'Agency' one time and ally myself with you."

Ally yourself with Nagato, not me.

"Under those circumstances, you would certainly be the first to back Nagato, so allying myself with you would be the equivalent of helping Nagato. Though my choice of wording may have been convoluted."

One side of his mouth twitched.

"Personally, I consider Nagato to be an important fellow member. I will want to stand by Nagato's side this one time should it be necessary. I may be a member of the 'Agency,' but I am first and foremost the deputy brigade chief of the SOS Brigade."

Koizumi was giving me a rather patronizing look. A look that seemed to suggest that he was satisfied and abandoning his right to speak his mind, now that his turn was over. In that case, I won't hesitate to do as I please.

Back in the middle of December—I'd been the only person left behind in a strange world, and after a considerable amount of running around, I'd managed to make my escape. The difference was that the rest of the SOS Brigade was here with me this time. No need for a Dragon Palace. We wouldn't be the ones disappearing. This space would.

I placed the blocks into their appropriate slots without any hesitation.

Click. I heard a satisfying sound. The sound of something metallic being lifted.

I held my breath and grabbed the doorknob. Then I focused all my strength.

The door slowly began to move.

"——"

I've been through a number of experiences that left me making sounds that couldn't be considered human speech. Whether it was from shock and disbelief or complete awe, there have been many times when I found myself thinking, "You've gotta be kidding me." I had figured that after being churned through space and time again and again, I would have developed a resistance—like how cockroaches become immune to bug spray.

But it appears that I'll have to strike that idea.

As soon as the heavy door finished opening—

"——"

—I found myself in a situation where I couldn't make any sound.

I couldn't believe my own eyes. Why would my optic nerves send such images to my brain? Did something go wrong? My retinas or lenses had gone out of whack or something?

The blinding sunlight made me dizzy. Bright rays of sunshine shone above.

"—The hell…"

The skies were so clear that I almost sneezed. There wasn't a single snowflake to be seen, let alone a howling blizzard. Blue skies stretched as far as the eye could see, without a speck of cloud in sight. There were only…

Lift cables obstructing the view. I could see a couple dressed in skiwear riding the clattering lift.

I staggered, as my legs felt heavier than they should.

There was snow. I was standing in snow. The sparkling white landscape only served to make me dizzier.

I sensed someone coming and looked up to see a figure glide right past me at breakneck speed.

"Wha?!"

I jumped reflexively and followed the figure with my eyes. It was a skier who had avoided me like I was an obstacle, wearing carving skis.

"This is…"

The ski slope. No doubt about it. A casual glance immediately revealed that there were skiers all around, enjoying themselves.

I looked around. The weight I felt on my shoulders belonged to the skis and poles I was carrying. I looked down at my feet to find that I was wearing ski boots. And I was dressed in the skiwear I had been allotted when leaving the Tsuruya vacation home.

I quickly turned to look behind me.

"Ah…?"

Asahina's mouth was open like a baby carp's as she blinked rapidly.

"Wow."

Koizumi was looking up at the sky in amazement. Naturally, they were both dressed in their skiwear, not T-shirts.

The mansion was nowhere to be found. In fact, it no longer existed. We were in the middle of a little-known ski slope. No sign at all of any uncharted, suspicious-looking mansions.

…Which meant…

"Yuki?!"

I heard Haruhi's voice come from up ahead as I turned my head and eyes in a rush.

Haruhi was holding up Yuki, who had apparently been lying on the snow.

"Are you okay? Yuki, is your fever…huh?"

Haruhi glanced around the way a pika would after exiting its burrow.

"That's odd…We were inside the mansion a moment ago."

Then she noticed me.

"Kyon, something about this feels weird…"

I didn't answer as I dumped my skis and poles and knelt down next to Nagato. Haruhi and Nagato were wearing the same clothes as when they'd been dashing down the slopes.

"Nagato."

My call was met by her short hair's rustling ever so slightly as she slowly lifted her head.

"…"

Two big eyes on a face completely void of emotion looked up at me, same as always. Nagato's face was covered with snow as her gaze fixated on my face for a bit.

"Yuki!"

Haruhi knocked me out of the way as she grabbed onto Nagato.

"I have no idea what's going on. But… Yuki, are you awake? Do you still have a fever?"

"No."

Nagato responded in a flat voice as she stood up on her own.

"I merely tripped."

"Really? But you have a terrible fever… or so I thought, but huh?"

Haruhi placed a hand against Nagato's forehead.

"You're right. It's gone. But."

She looked around our surroundings.

"Huh? The blizzard… Mansion… No way. It couldn't have been… a dream. What? Was it… a dream?"

Don't ask me. I don't provide reasonable answers. Not when you're the one asking the questions.

I feigned ignorance as I heard voices calling in the distance.

"What's up?"

I could see two figures waving their hands from the bottom of the slope.

"Mikuru! Harls!"

It was Tsuruya. Next to her were three snowmen of different sizes, and the other figure stood next to the medium-size one, which happened to be of similar height. Jumping up and down was my sister.

I was able to reestablish our current position.

The five of us were gathered a short distance from the lift station below the beginner's course.

"Well, whatever."

Haruhi apparently gave up on thinking about it.

"Yuki, I'll carry you, so get on my back."

"I am fine," said Nagato.

"You're not," Haruhi objected. "I don't really know what happened or why I'm so confused, but I'm not going to let you overexert yourself. You don't have a fever, but I just have a feeling that you're unwell. You need rest!"

Haruhi didn't wait for an answer before hoisting Nagato on her back and running off toward Tsuruya and my sister, who were still waving at us. She was probably going faster than a brand-new snowplow. Haruhi was going so fast that if there were a piggyback 100-meter dash event in the Winter Olympics, she'd be guaranteed gold.

Afterward.

Tsuruya contacted Arakawa, who picked us up in his car.

Nagato, in protest against Haruhi's treating her like a sick person, attempted to convince us that she was in good health, but the looks I gave her must have had some effect, as she eventually shut up and did as Haruhi said.

Nagato, Haruhi, Asahina, and my sister got in the car to return to the vacation home first, which left Koizumi, Tsuruya, and me to walk back on foot.

During that time, I engaged in conversation with Tsuruya.

"Say, I saw you guys walking down the slope and carrying your skis. What was up with that?"

Uh, there was a blizzard?

"Hmm? Oh, there were, like, ten minutes of heavy snowfall, I guess? But it wasn't that bad. Just a quick flurry out of nowhere, yeah?"

It appeared that we had spent hours walking around in the snow and relaxing in the mansion while only a few minutes had passed for Tsuruya.

Tsuruya continued with a brisk pace and tone.

"When I saw the five of you just scooting your way down, I was like, why? And then Nagato, leading the way, took a tumble. She got right back up, though."

Koizumi could only smile weakly as he kept his mouth shut. I did the same. So that was how we had appeared to an outside observer, in this case Tsuruya. And that was probably correct. We had been in some kind of dream or illusory world. This was reality, the original world.

After walking along in silence for a while, Tsuruya chuckled and moved her mouth next to my ear.

"Hey, Kyon. On a different note."

What's up, ma'am?

"I can tell from looking that Mikuru and Nagato aren't exactly normal. And Harls wouldn't be considered normal either!"

I stared at Tsuruya and discovered that the cheerful look on her face was genuine.

"You noticed?"

"Long, long time ago. But I don't know what they actually do! But they're doing some funny stuff behind the scenes, right? Ah, keep this a secret from Mikuru. She thinks that she's acting like an ordinary person!"

She must have found the look on my face amusing, as she doubled over and laughed heartily.

"Yep! But you're normal, Kyon. You and I are the same in that sense."

And then she peered at my face.

"Welp! I'm not going to ask about Mikuru's identity! Probably hard to answer! Doesn't really matter. We're still friends!"

… Haruhi, forget about the junior brigade member or honorary advisor stuff. Recruit Tsuruya as an official member. She's probably more perceptive than I am and better at playing the role of an ordinary person.

Tsuruya whacked me on the shoulder repeatedly.

"Take care of Mikuru. If she's ever troubled by something that she can't talk to me about, help her out!"

Well… but of course.

"Still."

Tsuruya's eyes were shining.

"That movie you made for the cultural festival. Was that actually based on a true story?"

I wasn't sure if Koizumi heard her, but I could see him shrugging off to the side.

When we arrived back at the vacation home, Haruhi had already forced Nagato into bed.

Her pale complexion was no longer dazed like it'd been in the mansion. She now had the same cool demeanor as when she was reading in the clubroom. I could even sense microscopic shifts in emotion. The Nagato we know and love.

Asahina and Haruhi were standing next to Nagato's bed like enchanting nurses while my sister and Shamisen were also standing by. I guess that they were waiting for us to arrive, because Haruhi began to talk once we were all assembled.

"Say, Kyon. I have a feeling that I had this strangely realistic dream. We went to a mansion, took a bath, and made some hot sandwiches to eat."

I was about to say that she'd been hallucinating, but Haruhi continued.

"Yuki said that she didn't know anything, but Mikuru remembered the same things I did."

I glanced over at Asahina. The lovely tea-serving maid looked down apologetically.

This is a problem. I was hoping to convince her that she'd been hallucinating or daydreaming, but I wasn't going to come up with a reasonable explanation for why two people had the same daydream anytime soon.

I was trying to figure out how I might trick her when I was interrupted.

"Group hypnosis."

Koizumi gave me an exaggerated look of exasperation as he cut in.

"In fact, I also vaguely remember something similar."

"You're saying that you were hypnotized? And I was too?" Haruhi asked.

"This was slightly different from artificial hypnotism, but yes. Knowing you, if a person were to announce that they were going to hypnotize you, you would become skeptical and the hypnosis would most likely fail."

"You're probably right."

Haruhi appeared to be lost in thought for a moment.

"However, we spent a considerable amount of time walking through the blizzard at a fixed rhythm where we could only see white snow. Are you aware of a phenomenon known as highway hypnosis? If you drive along a straight highway for an extended period of time, the evenly spaced lights can place the driver in a state of hypnosis and lull him to sleep. People often fall asleep while riding the train, and that's attributed to the rhythmic shaking of the cars. It's the same reasoning as when you pat a baby on its back to induce sleep."

"Really?"

The look on Haruhi's face suggested that she'd never heard of that before, while Koizumi nodded solemnly.

"Really."

His voice took on a persuasive tone.

"As we made our way through the blizzard, someone must have grumbled about wishing there was a mansion we could hide out in that provided all sorts of comforts...something along those lines. After all, we were enduring extreme conditions at the time that left us in a mental state that would be susceptible to such hallucinations. You've heard about people wandering through the desert and seeing mirages of oases, yes?"

Damn Koizumi. He's laying it on real thick.

"Uh-huh...I guess. So you're saying that we experienced something similar?"

Haruhi tilted her head and looked at me.

Apparently so. I nodded in an attempt to look convinced. Koizumi saw this as the perfect time to add the finishing touches.

"The sound of Nagato falling brought us back to our senses. I'm sure of it."

"Now that you mention it..."

Haruhi tilted her head even farther before swinging it back.

"Well, you're probably right. It wouldn't make sense for them to build a weird mansion out there, and my memory's becoming hazy. Like I was dreaming within a dream."

Yes, it was a dream. A mansion that didn't exist in reality. An unnecessary hallucination born of fatigue.

I was more worried about the other two members. The outsiders who weren't members of the SOS Brigade. I looked at Tsuruya.

"Heh!"

Tsuruya winked at me and smiled. I interpreted the look on her face as meaning, "Well, we'll just leave it at that." Though I may have been reading too much into it. Tsuruya didn't say another word as she flashed her trademark smile and refrained from any superfluous comments.

As for the other one, my sister, she was having sweet dreams from her position leaning into Asahina's lap. Like a cat, she was obnoxious when awake, but rather adorable when asleep. Asahina didn't seem to mind as she watched my sister's face. From the looks of things, I would guess that Asahina and my sister didn't hear the latter half of Koizumi's explanation.

Shamisen was grooming himself on the floor as he looked up at me and meowed. It was almost like he was trying to comfort me.

And when all was said and done, we finally reached the first night of our winter trip.

Nagato was apparently dying to get out of bed, but Haruhi would make a fuss every time by pushing her back down and throwing the covers over her.

I had a thought. There wasn't any need to force her to sleep. Even if she were to have fun dreams, they would still only be dreams. What mattered was that we were all here together right now. It didn't matter how wonderful a dream was if it ended the moment you woke up. I had no interest in transient illusions. This I understood—

A number of issues had been set aside. Like the identity of that mansion or whether Haruhi truly believed Koizumi's fib. Right now she was busy playing with Nagato so she didn't really care, it seemed.

I headed outside for no real reason, maybe to escape Haruhi's piercing voice. The night sky was filled with more stars than you'd ever see in the city and the reflected light made for a brilliant expanse of silver. Yet for some reason, I didn't feel cold at all.

"But."

Tomorrow would be the last day of the year. Koizumi's detective show would unfold on New Year's Eve, and Haruhi was planning on partying like crazy.

In that case, we might as well relax. I doubt that Nagato had been given many opportunities to kick back. I wasn't sure how much sleep she usually got or if she even needed to sleep, but she might as well use this chance to get her fill. Throwing Shamisen onto her bed was also a brilliant idea. He could serve as a source of heat.

I looked across the endless field of snow as I talked to myself.

"Doesn't look like we'll have a blizzard tonight."

I could only hope that if Nagato was capable of dreaming, she would be granted sweet dreams on this one night.

After all, I had absolutely no reason to wish otherwise.

I also took this opportunity to pray to the stars. It wasn't Tanabata, and it wasn't even New Year's Eve for that matter, but I wasn't specifically directing this prayer to Vega or Altair. Look at all the stars out there. I'm sure that my words will reach one of them.

"Make the new year a good one."

I'm counting on you, whoever's out there.

AFTERWORD

"ENDLESS EIGHT"

When I first wrote this story, it came out to exactly one hundred pages of draft paper. Twenty or so pages were trimmed for the version that was published in *The Sneaker*. I've taken this opportunity to revert to the original version. There weren't any major differences to speak of, but I must admit that it just felt better this way.

"THE DAY OF SAGITTARIUS"

On a tangent, I should mention that I have done very little gaming, and even less naming of games. I would consider beating one game a year an accomplishment. Incidentally, the most recent game that I managed to finish was Linda[3] Again. It was fun.

I'm thinking about getting a Dreamcast at some point.

"SNOWY MOUNTAIN SYNDROME"

This novella was completed recently. It's the longest short story I've done. I've found myself doing some serious research on where I might find an editing tool that automatically shortens your work.

I used the following books as references when writing this story. Many thanks.

- *Fermat's Enigma: The Epic Quest to Solve the World's Greatest Mathematical Problem* by Simon Singh, translated by Kaoru Aoki, published by Shinchosha
- *Fun with Shapes* by Eichi Ono, published by Iwanami Junior

Furthermore, I should add that any issues with the formulas and explanations used in the story can be blamed on an intellectual deficiency on my part.

Lastly, I would like to offer my condolences.

On July 15, 2004, Mr. Sunao Yoshida passed away.

Looking back, the first meeting with my esteemed colleague came during Kadokawa Shoten's spring event, right after the ceremony where I was awarded the grand prize at the Sneaker Awards. It had only been ten days since I had received a phone call about the award and quite frankly, I was just an amateur at the time. As an amateur, I could only follow my editor around and respectfully greet the renowned authors.

And as my nerves were reaching their limit, a cheerful man walked over slowly. He had a lively smile on his face as he slapped me on the shoulder.

"Hey, new kid!"

That man was Mr. Sunao Yoshida.

Hey, new kid. His words were as precise and clear as one could ever expect.

Afterward we exchanged a few snippets of conversation, during which I could only offer stiff, single-syllable responses. Despite that, he was still smiling at the end.

"Then I'll see you around."

And with that, he left. That would be the first and last time I ever met him.

I spent the next three days in bed with the flu, and once I recovered I decided that I should have provided better responses during our conversation. With that in mind, I prepared a few words to say if I ever had the chance to meet him again.

In the end, I forever lost my chance to tell him those words. However, I believe that they will not be wasted if I use this opportunity to say them.

I have long waited for the day when I could call out to him so.

"Hey, old-timer!"

Right now, I can only pray for his soul.

THE RAMPAGE OF
HARUHI SUZUMIYA

Illustration by Noizi ITO